"'Opping!" he said.

"You're a liar!" retorted the small girl, sharply.

"Ho!" said the boy. "Shows what you know about it."

"No, but," she said, admiringly, "'ave you though, straight?"

"I've bin at Yaldin'," he said, with immeasurable importance,—"at Yaldin' down in Kent for ite days. Me and another chap."

"Bin 'ome?" asked the girl, with interest.

"Not yet," he said. "When I do I shall 'ave to take a drop of something in for the old gel. I went off wifout letting her know and I expect she's been wonderin' what's become of me."

"Then if you ain't bin 'ome," said the little girl, breathlessly, "p'raps you don't—"

A strong voice called from a doorway.

"Trixie Bell! Trixie Bell! You come in this minute and look after the shop, you good-for-nothing little terror."

"I must be off," said the small girl, going hurriedly. "Wait 'ere till I come out again and I'll tell you somefing."

"I don't waste my time loafin' about for gels," said Master Lancaster, as the girl disappeared in a doorway. "Ketch me!"

He sauntered down the court towards Pitfield Street and, noting the crowd, slightly increased his pace. Taking a shilling from his coat pocket he tied it in a blue handkerchief and stuffed the handkerchief inside his waistcoat, being aware apparently that it is in a London crowd that property sometimes changes hands in the most astonishing manner.

"Very well then," said a fiery faced woman, who, getting the worst of an argument, was looking around for another subject, "if you did 'ave an uncle who was drowned, that's no reason why you should step on this little kid's toes."

"Born clumsy!" agreed Master Lancaster, resentfully rubbing his boot.

"Stand a bit aside, can't you, and let the youngster pass. 'Aving a uncle who was in the navy don't entitle you to take up all the room.

"Likely as not the little beggar's a witness and wants to go upstairs." The fiery faced woman looked down at the boy. "Are you a witness, dear?"

"Course I'm a witness," he said, readily.

"What did I tell you?" exclaimed the beefy faced woman with triumph. "Constable, 'ere 's a witness that 's got to be got upstairs. Make way for him, else he'll get hisself in a row for being late."

Whereupon, to his great amazement and satisfaction, Master Bobbie Lancaster found himself passed along through the thick crowd of matrons to the swing doors of the public-house; the importance of his mission being added to by every lady, so that when at last he reached the two policemen guarding the stairs he was introduced to them as a boy who saw the accident; could identify the driver, could, in short, clear up everything. Bobbie, accordingly, after being cuffed by the two policemen (more from force of habit than any desire to treat him harshly), was shot up the staircase past a window where, glancing aside, he saw the bunches of excited interested faces below; past a landing, and, the door being left momentarily unattended, he slipped into the room. He gave up instantly his newly gained character and crouched modestly in a corner behind the thirty members of the general public and kept his head well down.

"Now, now, now! Do let 's proceed in order. Is there any other witness who can throw any light on the affair? What?"

The club room of the public-house, with cider and whiskey advertisements on its brown papered walls, was long and narrow, and the stout genial man seated at the end of the table had command of the room from his position. He gave his orders to a bare-headed sergeant who hunted for witnesses and submitted the results at the other end of the long table; he smiled when he turned to the twelve moody gentlemen at the side of the table; to one, at the extreme end, who had a carpenter's rule in his breast pocket he was especially courteous. The carpenter made laborious notes with a flat lead pencil on a slip of blue paper, a proceeding at which the other members of the jury grunted disdainfully. Bobbie Lancaster, between the arms of two men in front of him, caught sight momentarily of the woman whom the sergeant had caught and who was now kissing the Testament. He recognised her as a neighbour.

"What does she say her name is, sergeant?"

"Mary Jane Rastin, sir."

"Mary Jane Rastin." The coroner wrote the name. "Very good! Now, Mrs. Rastin—"

"'Alf a minute," interrupted the carpenter. "Let me get this down right. W—r—a—"

"W be blowed," said the blowsy woman at the end of the table indignantly. "Don't you know how to spell a simple name like Rastin? Very clear you was before the days of the School Board."

"I have it down," said the coroner, suavely, "R—a—s—t—i—n."

"Ah," said Mrs. Rastin, in complimentary tones, "you're a gentleman, sir. You've had an education. You ain't been dragged up like—"

"Be careful what you're saying of," begged the carpenter, fiercely. "Don't you go aspersing my character, if you please. I'm setting 'ere now to represent the for and—"

"Now, now, my dear sir," said the coroner, "don't quarrel with the witness." He smiled cheerfully at the other members of the jury and almost winked. "That's my prerogative, you know." He turned to the

# A Son of the State by William Pett Ridge

William Pett Ridge was born at Chartham, near Canterbury, Kent on 22nd April 1859.

His family's resources were certainly limited. His father was a railway porter, and his son, after schooling in Marden, Kent became a clerk in a railway clearing-house. The hours were long and arduous, but self-improvement was his goal.  After working from nine until seven o'clock he attended evening classes at Birkbeck Literary and Scientific Institute and then he would write.

From 1891 his humourous sketches were published in the St James's Gazette, the Idler, Windsor Magazine and other literary periodicals of the day. He was heavily influenced by Dickens and critics thought he might be his successor.

Pett Ridge published his first novel in 1895, A Clever Wife. By his fifth novel, Mord Em'ly, three years later, his success was obvious.  His writing was written from the perspective of those born with no privilege and relied on talent to find humour and sympathy in his portrayal of working class life.

Today Pett Ridge and other East End novelists including Arthur Nevinson, Arthur Morrison & Edwin Pugh are grouped together as the Cockney Novelists.

With his success Pett Ridge gave generously of both time and money to charity. In 1907 he founded the Babies Home at Hoxton, one of several children's organisations

His circle considered Pett Ridge to be one of life's natural bachelors. In 1909 They were rather surprised therefore when he married Olga Hentschel.

As the 1920's arrived Pett Ridge added to his popularity with the movies. Four of his books were adapted into films.

Pett Ridge now found the peak of his fame had passed. He still managed to produce a book a year but was falling out of fashion and favour with the reading public.  His canon runs to over sixty novels and short-story collections as well as many pieces for magazines and periodicals.

William Pett Ridge died, on 29th September 1930, at his home, Ampthill, Willow Grove, Chislehurst, at the age of 71.

## Index of Contents

CHAPTER I

The round white September moon lighted up Pitfield Street from end to end, making the gas lights in the shop windows look abashed and unnecessary; out in the Old Street triangle, men on the wooden seats who had good eyesight read halfpenny evening papers as though it were day, able without trouble to make record in knowing-looking pocket-books of the running of Ormonde. At the Hoxton Theatre of Varieties, the early crowd streamed out into Pitfield Street flushed with two hours of joy for twopence, and the late crowd which had been waiting patiently for some time at the doors, flowed in. When these two crowds had disappeared, the Old Street end of Pitfield Street belonged once more to the men and women who were shopping, and at the obtrusive fruiterer's (with a shop that bulged almost to the kerb and a wife whose size was really beyond all reason), even there one could just pass without stepping into the road. Further up the street, outside a public-house, was, however, another crowd blocking the pathway, and this crowd overflowed into the dim passage by the side of the public-house, where it looked up at a lighted room on the first floor with an interest ungenerously repaid by the back view of a few heads. A grown-up crowd, mainly of middle-aged women. Children had given up efforts to belong to it, and down the passage, which was as the neck of a bottle leading into a court quite six feet wide, youngsters shouted and sang and quarrelled and played at games. From the direction of the other end came a short acute-faced boy with a peakless cap, a worn red scarf tied very tightly around his neck. He had both hands in the pockets of a jacket which was too large for him; he smoked the fag-end of a cigar with the frowning air of a connoisseur who is not altogether well pleased with the brand. He stopped, signalled with a jerk of his head to a slip of a girl who was disputing for the possession of an empty lobster can, with the vigour that could not have been exceeded if the lobster can had been a jewel case of priceless value; she retired at once from the struggle, and, pulling at her stocking, ran towards him.

"Where's all the chaps?" he asked, removing the cigar stump from his lips.

"Where've you bin, Bobbie Lancaster?" she asked, without replying to his question.

"You 'eard what I asted you, Trix," he said, steadily. "I asted you where all the chaps was."

"Some of 'em have gone over 'Ackney way," said the slip of a girl. "Where've you bin?"

He flicked the black ash from the fag end in the manner of one five times his age.

trembling lady at the end of the table. "Now, Mrs. Rastin, you live in Pimlico Walk, and you are, I believe, a widow?" Mrs. Rastin bowed severely, and then looked at the carpenter as who should say, What do you make of that, my fine fellow? The coroner went on. "And you knew the deceased?"

"Intimate, sir!"

"Was she a woman with—er, inebriate tendencies?"

"Pardon, sir?"

"I say was she a woman who had a weakness for alcohol?"

The sergeant interpreted, "Did she booze?"

"She liked her glass now and again, sir," said Mrs. Rastin, carefully.

"That is rather vague," remarked the coroner. "What does 'now and again' mean?"

"Well, sir," said Mrs. Rastin, tying the ribbons of her rusty bonnet into a desperate knot, "what I mean to say is whenever she had the chance."

"You were with her before the accident?"

"I were!"

"You had been drinking together?"

"Well, sir," said Mrs. Rastin, impartially, and untying her bonnet-strings, "scarcely what you'd call drinking. It was like this. It were the anniversary of my weddin' day, and, brute as Rastin always was, and shameful as he treated all my rel'tives in the way of borrowin', still it's an occasion that comes, as I say, only once a year, and it seems wicked not to take a little something special, if it's only a drop of—"

"And after you had been together some time, you walked along Haberdasher Street to East Street."

"With the view, sir," explained Mrs. Rastin, "of 'aving a breath of fresh air before turning in."

"Was the deceased the worse for drink?"

"Oh, no, sir! No, nothing of the kind." Mrs. Rastin was quite emphatic. "She felt much the better for it. She said so."

A corroborative murmur came from the crowd behind which Bobbie was hiding; one of the endorsements sounded so much like the tones of his mother that he edged a little further away. He had become interested in the proceedings, and after the great good fortune of getting into the room, he did not want to be expelled by an indignant parent.

"How was it you did not see the omnibus coming along?"

"Just one query I should like to ask first," interposed the carpenter, holding up his left hand with a dim remembrance of school etiquette. "What time was all this?"

"Six o'clock, as near as I can remember," snapped Mrs. Rastin.

"Six o'clock in the morning?" asked the carpenter, writing.

"No, pudden head," said Mrs. Rastin, contemptuously. "Six o'clock in the evening. Why don't you buy a new pair of ears and give another twopence this time and get a good—All right, sir." To the coroner. "I'll answer your question with pleasure. I know when I'm speaking to gentlemen, and I know when I'm talking to pigs." Mrs. Rastin glanced triumphantly at the carpenter, and the carpenter looked appealingly at his unsympathetic colleagues in search of support. "We was standing on the kerb as I might be 'ere. Over there, as it might be, where the young man in glasses is that's connected with the newspaper, was a barrer with sweetstuff. 'Oh!' she says all at once, 'I must get some toffee,' she says, 'for my little boy 'gainst he comes 'ome,' she says. With that, and before I could so much as open me mouth to say 'Mind out!' the poor deer was 'alf way across the road; the 'bus was on her and down she went. I cuts across to her"—Mrs. Rastin wept, and Bobbie could hear responsive sobs from the women near him—"I cuts across to her, and she says. 'I—I never got the sweets for him,' she says. Thinking of her—of her little boy right at the last; you understand me, sir! And the constable off with his cape and put it under her 'ead, and she just turned, and," Mrs. Rastin wept bitterly, "and it was all over." Mrs. Rastin patted her eyes with a deplorable handkerchief. "'Yes,' she says, 'I never got them sweets—'"

"Pardon me!" said the carpenter. "Did you make a note of them words at the time? What I mean to say is, did you write 'em down on paper?"

"Not being," said Mrs. Rastin, swallowing, her head shivering with contempt, and speaking with great elaboration, "not being a clever juggins with a miserable twopenny 'apenny business as joiner and carpenter in 'Oxton Street, and paying about a penny in the pound, if that, I did not write them words down on paper."

"Ho!" said the carpenter, defiantly. "Then you ought to 'ave."

Mrs. Rastin was allowed to back from the end of the table and to take a privileged seat on a form where she had for company the witnesses who had already given evidence. These were an anxious 'bus driver, a constable of the G Division, and a young doctor from the hospital. The sergeant went hunting again in the crowd, and this time captured what appeared to be a small girl, but proved to be a tiny specimen of a mature woman. Bobbie Lancaster, dodging to get a sight of her, chuckled as he recognized Miss Threepenny (so called from some fancied resemblance to that miniature coin), a little person whom he had not infrequently derided and chased.

"I really don't know that we want any more evidence, sergeant," remarked the coroner. "What do you say, gentlemen?"

Eleven of the gentlemen replied that they had had ample; the carpenter waited until they had stated this, and then decided that the little woman's evidence should be heard. Miss Threepenny, stepping on tiptoe, her hands folded on the handle of a rib-broken umbrella that was for her absurdly long, explained that she saw the accident, being then on her way home from her work at a theatrical costumier's in Tabernacle Street.

"I was on the point of crossing the road, your worship," said the tiny woman in her shrill voice, "jest 'esitatin' on the kerb, when I see the 'bus coming along, and I says to myself, 'I'll wait till this great 'ulking thing goes by,' I says, 'and then I'll pop across.' The thought," said Miss Threepenny, dramatically, "had no sooner entered my mind than across the road runs the poor creature, under the 'orses' 'eels she goes, and I,—well, I went off into a dead faint."

The mite of a creature looked round the room as though anticipating commendation for her appropriate behaviour.

"And you agree with the other witnesses, my good little girl, that—"

"Excuse me," interrupted Miss Threepenny, with great dignity, "I'm not a good little girl; I'm a grown-up woman of thirty-three."

"Thirty what?" asked the carpenter, his pencil ready to record facts.

"Thirty-three," she repeated, sharply.

A confirmatory murmur came from the crowd of women at the back of the room. The sergeant told the women to be quiet.

"My mistake," said the coroner, politely, and waving aside the incredulous carpenter. "The point is—you think it was an accident, don't you, madam?"

"It were an accident," said Miss Threepenny, looking round and fixing the nervous 'bus driver with her bright, black little eyes, "that would never have happened if drivers on 'busses was to attend to their business instead of having their heads turned and carrying on conversation with long silly overgrown gels riding on the front seat."

The little woman, having made this statement, kissed the Testament again as though to make doubly sure, and, with an air of dignity that no full-grown woman would ever have dared to assume, trotted off to take her seat next the 'bus driver. On the 'bus driver whispering something viciously behind his hand, Miss Threepenny replied with perfect calm in an audible voice that it was no use the 'bus driver flirting with her, for she was a strict Wesleyan.

The carpenter's obstinacy necessitated the clearing of the court now that the time had arrived for the jury to consider their verdict, and Master Lancaster, much to his annoyance, found himself borne out of the room in the middle of the crowd of women. He doubted the probability of getting back into the room to hear the verdict, because it seemed scarce likely that he would again have the good luck to slip in unobserved by the policeman at the door. He went to the first landing and looked out on the upturned faces in the court below. A long youth with pince-nez, who had been taking notes upstairs, came down, and, in opening an evening paper, brushed unintentionally against Bobbie's face.

"That's my dial," said the boy, truculently, "when you've done with it."

"I'm sorry," said the young reporter.

"You're clumsy," said Bobbie.

"What are you doing at an affair of this kind?"

"Answerin' silly questions what are put to me." The reporter laughed, and, striking a match, lighted a cigarette. "After you," said Bobbie, producing another fag-end of a cigar, "after you with the match."

"Like smoking?" asked the young man.

"Perfect slive to it," said the boy, puffing the smoke well away in a manner that belied the assertion.

"Queer little beggar!" said the young man. "Where d'you live?"

"'Ome!" said the boy, promptly. "Where d'you think, cloth-head?"

"Strictly speaking," remarked the youth, with good humour, "my name is not cloth-head. My name is Myddleton West."

"Can you sleep a-nights?" asked the boy, "with a name like that?"

"Myddleton West, journalist, of 39, Fetter Lane, Holborn. Now tell me yours."

The boy complied reluctantly. With decreasing hesitation he gave further particulars.

"I'll do a sketch about you," said Myddleton West, looking down at the boy. "'The Infant of Hoxton' I think I'll call it."

"Going to put some'ing about me in the paper?" asked the boy, with undisguised interest, and discarding entirely his attitude of defiance.

"If they'll take it. There is at times a certain coyness on the part of editors—"

The boy suddenly started. He touched the brass rod, and flew downstairs with so much swiftness that he reached the court before Myddleton West had discovered his absence. West looked up and saw the constable descending to call him back to the room; the reason for Bobbie Lancaster's flight became obvious.

The boy slipped eel-like through the crowd of women at the doorway, and presently reached moonlight and Hoxton Street, where he drifted intuitively to the outside of the theatre. It gratified him exceedingly as he felt the shilling in his knotted handkerchief, to think that he might, if he were so minded—the hour being now half-past eight—go in at half price, and seating himself in the stage box, witness the last three acts of "Foiled by a Woman." He laughed outright as, standing near the lamps, he looked in at the swing doors of the principal entrance and imagined the astonishment of those in the three-penny gallery, high up on the top of the mountain of faces within, were they to see him enter importantly the box at the right of the stage and survey with lordly air the crowded, heated, interested house. How they would roar at him if he were to stick a penny in his eye and, carefully stroking an imaginary moustache, say, "Bai Jove! What people!" It would not be the first time that he had amused a crowd; once at a fire in Shoreditch he had put on a paper helmet, pretending to be chief of the fire brigade, and a matron in the crowd, watching him, had been so exceptionally amused at his antics that she had had to be unlaced and dragged home by solicitous lady friends. The boy resisted the temptations of the enticing placards, for he had already decided on the manner in which the shilling was to be expended; the recollection of this made him think of home. There would be some argument, he knew, with his mother concerning his long absence, but, once the first storm was over, sunshine would come, and a small flask and sausages would make her content.

He stepped in at the dark open doorway of his home, and went upstairs. At the end of the passage on the ground floor a smelly oil lamp diffused scent, but not light; it served only to accentuate the blackness. The boy knew the stairs well, and dodging the hole on the fifth stair and stepping over the eighth—the eighth was a practical joke stair, and if you stepped on its edge it instantly stood up and knocked your leg—he piloted himself adroitly on the landing. There were voices in the back room.

"Comp'ny!" said Bobbie. "So much the better."

He pushed the door and entered. Two women in a corner, examining the contents of a crippled chest of drawers by the aid of a candle, looked affrightedly over their shoulders.

"Ullo!" said Bobbie. "What's your little game?"

"You give us quite a turn, Bobbie," said Mrs. Rastin nervously, "coming in so quiet. Where 'ave you bin all this time, deer?"

"Where's the old gel?" asked Bobbie, taking his parcels from his pocket. "Where's she got to?"

"'Eaven," said Mrs. Rastin's friend, trying to close the drawer.

"Don't try to be funny," advised the boy, "you can't do it well, and you'd better be 'alf leave it alone. How long 'fore she'll be in?"

"You 'aven't 'eard, deer," said Mrs. Rastin, coming forward and taking the flask from him absently. "Your poor mother's bin run over and we've jest bin 'olding her inquest."

Bobbie Lancaster sat down on the wooden chair and blinked stupidly at the two women.

"And was that—was that my old gel that you give evidence about jest now up at the—"

"Yes, Bobbie. That was your poor dear mother, and a lovinger heart never breathed. Not in this world at any rate." Mrs. Rastin uncorked the flask and sniffed at it. "But you must cheer up, you know, because it was to be, and all flesh is grass, and we shall meet, please God—" Mrs. Rastin took a sip.

"And there's many a kid," chimed in the other neighbour, "that's just as bad off as you, my lad, losing both their parents, and you mustn't think you're the only one, ye know. You want a glass, Mrs. Rastin."

The boy did not cry. His mouth twitched slightly, and he frowned as though endeavouring to understand clearly the position of affairs.

"Old man died," he said slowly, "soon after I was born, and now the old gel's gone."

"Yes, Bobby! Run and get a lump of sugar, Mrs. What-is-it, out of my caddy."

"So," said the boy, "it 'mounts to this. I ain't got no fawther and I ain't got no mother."

"That's about it, Bobbie."

The boy jerked his chin and commenced to unlace his boots rather fiercely.

"Dem bright look out for me," he said.


## CHAPTER II

The boy's sense of injury gave way, and became, indeed, utterly routed the next morning by a feeling of importance. Mrs. Rastin bustled in and prepared a breakfast that filled the room with a most entrancing scent of frying fish; to show her sympathy she sat down with him to the meal, and ate with excellent appetite, beguiling the time with cheery accounts of sudden deaths and murders and suicides that she, in the past, had had the rare good fortune to encounter. Mrs. Rastin took charge of the keys belonging to the chest of drawers, remarking that so far as regarded any little thing that Bobbie's poor dear mother might have left, she would see that right was done just the same as though it were her own. Holidays being on at the Board School which Bobbie intermittently attended, Mrs. Rastin said how would it be if he were to take a turn in Hoxton Street for a few hours whilst she turned to and tidied up?

"Jest as you like," said Bobbie agreeably.

"Don't you go and get into no mischief, mind," counselled Mr. Rastin.

"Trust me," said the boy.

"Keep away from that Shoreditch set, and take good care of yourself. You're all alone in the world now," said Mrs. Rastin, pouring the last drop from the teapot into her cup, "and you'll 'ave to look out. You 'ain't got no mother to 'elp you."

"By-the-bye," said Bobbie, "who's going to cash up for putting the old woman away?"

"Me and a few neighbours are going to see to it," remarked the lady with reserve. "Don't you bother your 'ead about that. Run off and—Just a minute, I'll sew this black band round the sleeve of your coat."

"Whaffor?" asked the boy.

"Why, bless my soul!" exclaimed Mrs. Rastin. "As a sign that you're sorry, of course.'

"That's the idea, is it?"

"Some one'll 'ave to buy you a collar, too, for Tuesday."

"Me in a collar?" he said gratified. "My word, I shall be a reg'lar toff, if I ain't careful."

"What size—I think that'll hold—what size do you take, I wonder?"

"Lord knows," said the boy. "I don't. I've never wore one yet."

If in Hoxton that day a more conceited boy than Robert Lancaster had been in request, the discovery would have been difficult. He strolled up and down Hoxton Street, where the second-hand furniture dealers place bedsteads brazenly in the roadway, and when shop people, standing at their doors, glanced at the crape band on his sleeve he stood still for a while in order that they might have a good view.

A good-natured Jewess in charge of a fruit stall called to him and inquired the nature of his loss, and on Bobbie supplying the facts (adding to the interest by various details suggested by his imagination) the Jewess gave an enormous sigh and, as token of sympathy, presented him with two doubtful pears and a broken stick of chocolate. Bobbie went up towards New North Road inventing further details of a gruesome nature, in the hope of finding other shopkeepers similarly curious and appreciative, but no one else called to him, and at a confectioner's shop, where he waited for a long time, a girl with her hair screwed by violent twists of paper came out and said that if he did not leave off breathing on their window she would wring his neck for him; upon Bobbie giving her a brief criticism in regard to the arrangement of her features, she repeated her threat with increased emphasis, and as there was obviously nothing to be gained by further debate, he strolled off with dignity through Fanshaw Street, arriving presently at Drysdale Street. The boys here were boys with an intolerably good opinion of themselves, because they lived in a street over which the railway passed; this made them hold themselves aloof from the other youths of Hoxton, and go through life with the austerity of men who knew the last word about engines. It seemed to Bobbie Lancaster that a chance had now arisen to humiliate Drysdale Street and to lower its pride.

"Cheer!" he said casually.

"Cheer!" said the two boys. They were marking out squares on the pavement for a game of hop-scotch. "Got any more chalk in your pocket, Nose?"

The boy called Nose searched, and shook his head negatively. "Daresay I can oblige you," remarked Bobbie.

"Look 'ere," said the first boy with heated courtesy, "did anyone ast you come 'ere standin' on our pavement?"

"No," acknowledged Bobbie.

"Very well, then! You trot off 'fore you get 'urt.

"Who you going to get to 'urt me?" asked Bobbie.

"Going to get no one," said the first boy aggressively. "Going to do it meself."

"I should advise you to go into training a bit first," said Bobbie kindly. "Them arms and wrists of yours I should sell for matches; your boots you might get rid of as sailin' vessels."

"'Old my jacket, Nose," said the boy furiously. "I'll knock the stuffin' out of him 'fore I'm many minutes older."

"With a shirt like yourn," said Bobbie, edging back a little, "I should keep me jacket on. You'll frighten all the birds."

"You'd better be off," said Nose, feeling it safe now to offer a remark. "Come down 'ere temorrer, and we'll spoil your face for you."

"Take a bit o' doin' to spoil yourn," shouted Bobbie.

"Come down temorrer," repeated Nose defiantly, "and I'll give you what for."

"Make it the next day," called Bobbie. "I shall be at the cimetry temorrer."

"Cimetry?" said the two boys with a change of voice.

"Cimetry!" repeated Master Lancaster with pride.

"Who is it?"

"Mother," said Bobbie.

"Come 'ere," said the first boy putting on his jacket. "Tell us all about it."

"Fen punchin'," requested Bobbie cautiously.

"Fen punchin'," agreed the two Drysdale Street boys.

Such was the respect Bobbie exacted from the two boys during the truce and after his recital, that they not only allowed him to lose a game of hop-scotch with them, but at his urgent request they took him to the railway arch, and permitted him to climb to a place where, when a train presently went shrieking overhead, a thunderous noise came to his ears that deafened him. The thin boy's name was George Libbis; the other boy's name it appeared was not really Nose but Niedermann; called Nose for brevity, and because that feature was unusually prominent. With Master Libbis, Bobbie presently found himself on good terms; with Nose he had, before saying good-bye, a brief tussle over the possession of a piece of string, and went off with a truculent remark concerning German Jews.

He felt so much advanced in society by reason of this entrance into Drysdale Street circles that he declined games with boys of Pimlico Walk, and affected not to see Trixie Bell dancing a neighbour's baby that was not quite so large as herself, but more muscular. Trixie called after him peremptorily, but he went by with his head well up and eyes alert for signs of interest. In Charles Square his reserve was broken by sudden encounter with Ted Sullivan. Master Sullivan, in possession of a toy pistol with small paper caps that snapped quite loudly, told Bobbie in confidence that he had half made up his mind to get a mask and go out somewhere and stop the mail coach, shoot the driver, and take all the gold and bank-notes that it carried. Upon Bobbie inquiring where he proposed to find this mail coach, shoot the driver, and take the bullion, Master Sullivan declared that there were plenty about if you only knew where to find them, and in confirmation exhibited the coloured paper cover of a well thumbed book, called "Dashing Dick Dare-devil, or the Highwayman and the Faithful Indian Girl," confronted with which evidence Bobbie Lancaster relinquished his argument and acknowledged that Ted Sullivan had reason. Because these adventures are not to be entered upon without rehearsal and taking thought, the two had a brief game round the tipsy railings of the old square; Bobbie starting from the county court was a restive steed conveying a stage coach which bore untold gold, and just as he galloped round by the untidy public-house at the north-west corner, who should rush out upon him but Master Sullivan with black dirt upon his face so that he should not be recognized, and presenting the toy pistol with a stern warning.

"Stir but a single step and I fire."

Upon which, the restive steed tried to gallop over the highwayman and to gallop round him, and eventually to turn and gallop back; the highwayman was just on the point of snapping his last cap and rendering the noble horse senseless when, most inopportunely, the highwayman's mother appeared at the corner.

"Teddy Sullivin! Come here, ye mis'rable little hound, and let me knock the head off of ye, ye onholy son of a good parint that ye are."

This interruption left the struggle at a highly interesting point, but Master Sullivan before leaving said that he proposed to get a proper revolver, some day, and then there would be larks of the rarest and most exciting kind. Meanwhile, added Master Sullivan as he went off, the watchword was "Death to Injuns!"

Bobbie, after a highly enjoyable morning, went home, where, thanks to Mrs. Rastin, the house reeked with a perfectly entrancing odour of frying steak and onions. To this meal Mrs. Rastin invited a lady from downstairs, called the Duchess, who wore several cheap rings and spoke with a tone of acquired refinement that had always impressed Bobbie very much. He remembered, though, that his mother had warned him never to speak to this lady from downstairs, and when that vivacious lady addressed him at his meal, he refused at first to answer her, thus forcing the conversation to be shared exclusively by the two ladies. They talked of rare tavern nights, the lady from downstairs shaking her head reminiscently as she re-called diverting incidents of the past, declaring that the world was no longer what it had been.

"Why, there's no Cremorne, now," argued the Duchess affectedly.

"True, true!" agreed Mrs. Rastin.

"Argyll Rooms, and the rest of it, all swept away," complained the Duchess.

"It's sickenin'," said Mrs. Rastin. "I s'pose they was rare times if the truth was known."

"You'd never believe?"

"Onfortunately," said Mrs. Rastin humbly, "I was country-bred meself. I wasted all the best years of my life in service down in Essex."

"Why, in my day," remarked the Duchess, smoothing the torn lace at her sleeves, "in my day I've sat at the same table with people that you couldn't tell from gentlefolk, thinking no more of champagne than we do of water."

"Goodness."

"Nobody never thought of walking," declared the Duchess ecstatically. "It was cabs here, cabs there, cabs everywhere."

"That's the way," said the interested Mrs. Rastin.

"Talk about sparkling conversation," said the Duchess with enthusiasm. "They can't talk like it now, that's a very sure thing."

"I don't know what's come over London," remarked Mrs. Rastin despairingly. "It's more like a bloomin' church than anything else. I s'pose you was a fine-looking young woman in those days, ma'am."

"I don't suppose," said the Duchess, "there was ever a finer."

The night of that day became so extended by reason of a generous supply of drink, that Bobbie went to bed in the corner of the room and left the two women still reviewing the days and nights that were. He understood their conversation imperfectly (although God knows there was little in the way of worldly knowledge hidden from him), but he decided that the Duchess was worthy of some respect as one who had moved in society, and when she stumbled over to him and kissed him, crooning a comic song as lullaby, he felt gratified. He remembered that his mother had kissed him once. It was when he was quite a child; at about the time that his father died. For the first time he found himself thinking of her, and his mouth twitched, but he bent his mind determinedly to the ride that he was to enjoy in the morning, and having persuaded himself that everything had happened for the best, went presently to sleep, content.

The journey the next morning proved indeed to be all that imagination had suggested, with a high wind added, with the manners of a hurricane. There was a new peaked cap for him to wear; the white collar was fixed with difficulty, being by accident some two sizes too large and bulging accordingly. Mrs. Rastin, swollen eyed partly with tears, assisted him to dress; herself costumed in black garments borrowed from opulent neighbours in the Walk.

A man appeared whom Bobbie recognized as the boy Nose's father, and he, glancing round the room, said depreciatingly that there was nothing there worth carting away, but Mrs. Rastin told him to look at the chest of drawers; to look at the bedstead; to look at the mirror. Mr. Niedermann, still contemptuous, said that if he gave fifteen bob for the lot he should look down on himself for being an adjective idiot; Mrs. Rastin reasoned strongly against this attitude, saying that she was quite sure that two pounds five would not hurt him. Mr. Niedermann intimated, with much emphasis, that, on the contrary, two pound five would do him very grievous injury, apart from the fact that, by offering that sum, he would be making himself the laughing-stock of all Hoxton.

A neighbour here looked in to announce that the carriage was waiting, and after a sharp argument, conducted with great asperity on both sides, Mrs. Rastin climbed down from two pounds five to one pound two-and-six, and Mr. Niedermann, with a generous flow of language that was in an inverse ratio to his manner of disbursing money, climbed up to that amount, and Mr. Niedermann's men came in and took everything away, leaving the room empty and bare. Mr. Niedermann paid over the amount, assuring Mrs. Rastin and Bobbie that a few jobs of similar character would bankrupt him, and departed, Mrs. Rastin acutely placing a small bag containing money under a loose plank of the flooring where, as she said to the Duchess, it would be, if anything, safer than in the Bank of England. The work completed, Mrs. Rastin showed them out and locked the door, placing the key under the mat. In Hoxton Street the carriage waited; the gloomy horses, standing with feet extended to avoid being blown away, turned round as the two came up through admiring rows of people as who should say, "Oh, you have come at last, then." The scarlet-faced driver and his colleague were rubbing marks of mud off the black carriage; Trixie Bell was there, and slipped a clammy piece of sweetstuff into Bobbie's hand as he was about to be lifted into the coach, which piece of sweetstuff he instantly threw away, to the regret of Trixie Bell and the joy of an infant at whose feet it was thrown, and who apparently thought the age of miracles had come again. The wind took off Bobbie's new cap, carrying it sportively into a puddle. Fifty people ran to recover it, and the cap came back with enough of the puddle to give it age. Mrs. Rastin occupied the journey, as the two gloomy horses trotted to the mortuary, with wise precepts, to the effect that boys who couldn't keep their new caps on, never by any dexterity or luck or artfulness went to Heaven. Bobbie did not mind this; he was too much interested in looking out of the window of the carriage. It seemed to him that it was like belonging to the royal family.

"'Ere we are, at the gates," said Mrs. Rastin, finding her handkerchief. "Now mind you cry and behave yourself properly like a good boy, or else, when I get you 'ome, I'll give you the best shakin' you ever had in all your born days."

"Don't upset yourself," said the boy.

"I'll upset you, me lord," retorted Mrs. Rastin. "You'll have to be knocked into shape a bit before you'll be good for anything; 'itherto you've been allowed to do too much jest as you bloomin' well pleased."

"Now who's behavin'?" asked Bobbie satirically. The carriage went slowly through the opened iron gates and up the broad gravelled walk. "Nice language to use in a churchyard, I don't think."

"It's your fault," said Mrs. Rastin.

"It's you that'll get punished for it," said the boy, "anyway."

"Another word," declared Mrs. Rastin strenuously, "and you don't get out of the kerrige."

"Try it on," said Bobbie, "if you dare."

As they had to wait some few minutes outside the chapel the purple-faced driver came round to the window and, holding his ruffled silk hat on, engaged Mrs. Rastin in conversation, mentioning casually that he knew a place where presently as good a glass of beer could be obtained as the heart desired. Mrs. Rastin, promising to remember this, mentioned that for the price, she thought it—meaning the coach and horses—by no means a bad turn-out. The purple-faced coachman took this compliment placidly, remarking that it was cutting it pretty adjective fine to do the thing for two pun two, and if it were his show he should decline to put the harness on the horses under two pun twelve. If people liked to go and die, said the coachman firmly, let them pay for it. On Mrs. Rastin remarking that she supposed it was what we must all come to, the coachman replied that Mrs. Rastin would be perfectly safe in laying all the money she had got on that.

"Now they're ready for us," said the coachman. And whistled to his colleague.

Bobbie, following the draped case, which was borne on the shoulders of the two men, felt full of regret that he had no audience; Mrs. Rastin, blown about distractedly by the tempestuous wind, appeared too much occupied to cry. The young curate, in his white surplice, wore a skull cap and looked resentfully at the elements as he spoke the opening words. The liturgy came to Bobbie's ears in detachments when the wind rested for a moment.

"I am the resurrection and the life, saith the Lord, he that believeth on me, though he were dead, yet. . . ."

"Lord, let me know mine end, and the number of my days. . . ."

"Oh spare me a little that I may recover my strength before I go hence and be no more seen. . . ."

The small procession moved to a shallow opening in the clay earth. The driver and his stolid companion let the long draped case down to the side of this opening, the driver complaining in an undertone of the other's clumsiness; as lief have a plank of wood to help him, growled the driver. The straps were placed round the long case; the boy watching had difficulty in preventing himself from offering a word of advice.

"Man that is born of woman hath but a short time to live. . . ."

"Suffer us not in our last hour from any pains of death to fall from Thee. . . ."

The stolid man picked up a lump of dry clay and crumbled it.

"Forasmuch as it hath pleased Almighty God of His great mercy to take unto Himself the soul of our dear sister here departed. . . ."

Presently a prayer that Bobbie knew. He muttered it by rote and without the least desire to consider the meaning of the words. "Our Fa'r, chart in 'Eaven, 'allowed be—" The curate closed the book and controlled his white surplice from the vagaries of the gusty irreverent wind.

"The grace of our Lord Jesus Christ, and the love of God, and the fellowship of the Holy Ghost, be with us all evermore. Amen."

"This the poor creature's son?" asked the young curate briskly and cheerfully.

"Her only boy, sir."

"And you are his aunt, eh?"

"No, sir! Only a well-meanin' neighbour; he ain't got any rel'tives, worse luck."

"So you're all alone in the world, my boy? (Bother the wind!) Now you must make up your mind to be a good lad, because there are plenty of people ready to help good lads, and very few who will waste their time over bad ones."

"That's what I tell him, sir," remarked Mrs. Rastin ingratiatingly.

"And don't forget—" The curate stopped and sneezed. "Enough to give anybody a cold," said he. "Good-bye, my lad."

"Say good-bye to the kind gentleman, Bobbie."

"So long," said Bobbie, resenting the interference of Mrs. Rastin. "Look after that cold of yourn."

"Nice thing to say, upon my word," declared Mrs. Rastin, manoeuvring the wind. "You've got no more idea of etiquette than a 'og. If it wasn't that your poor mother was lying down there, poor thing, I'd give you a jolly good 'iding."

"Let me ketch you trying at it," said Bobbie defiantly.

Thus, without a tear, the boy left the edge of the oblong hole in clay earth, and was blown back to the carriage. Though his eyes were dry and his manner aggressive, there came a regretful feeling now all the excitement was over, that he had to resume his position of an ordinary boy with no longer any special claims to respect in Hoxton. He wondered vaguely what the next few days would be like. He was not capable of looking beyond that. At the gate Mrs. Rastin alighted to patronise the house of refreshment so urgently recommended by the driver, and whilst that purple-faced gentleman conducted her to the private bar, Bobbie remained in the carriage, and the other man came round and looked stolidly in through the window without saying a word, as though Bobbie were a new arrival at the Zoo.

When Mrs. Rastin, in excellent humour, returned, she brought a seed biscuit for Bobbie, told him that he was a model boy, and that she wished there were six of him for her to look after.

"You run 'ome to your room," said Mrs. Rastin, when the carriage stopped in Hoxton Street, "the key's under the mat, and I shan't be many minutes 'fore I'm with you. Wait for me, there's a deer. I must have a drop of something short."

In the walk he was hailed.

"I say, Bobbie Lancaster."

"Now, what is it?"

"My mother says," began Trixie Bell, panting, "that you—."

"I don't talk to gels," said the boy, marching on.

"Says that you ain't in—."

"Be off, I tell you. Don't let me 'ave to speak twice."

"That you ain't in good 'ands where you are now."

"Ain't what?"

Miss Bell, persistent, repeated the statement.

"You'll pardon me," said the boy laboriously, "if I ast a rude question. Is your mother still kerryin' on her business?"

"She is," said Trixie.

"Very well, then," he said, going on, "tell her to jolly well mind it."

"She says they're a bad lot," shouted the girl, "and she says they won't do you no good."

"Don't make me come back and pull your 'air for you," entreated Bobbie.

"Cow—werd!" bawled Miss Trixie Bell.

"Cat!" shouted Mr. Robert Lancaster.

Looking back as be pressed open the black door, he saw the youth called Nose talking to the small girl, and he felt tempted to return and punish both of them, but it occurred to him that a man with a collar could not afford to appear undignified. He went upstairs. The key not being under the mat, he sat astride the rickety banisters and waited. He had found that morning a half emptied box of fusees, and the time did not seem long.

"Don't tell me the key ain't under the mat," said Mrs. Rastin truculently, as she came up the stairs. "You're too lazy to look for it; that's about the truth; you little—."

"Find it yourself, then."

"Why 'ere it is in the door," said Mrs. Rastin, "in the door all the time." She unlocked it. "Ain't you got no eyes, you good-for-nothing?" Mrs. Rastin stumbled over the mat and went into the dark room. "Light a match when I keep telling you."

In the room, Bobbie held up one of the flaming fusees. Mrs. Rastin blinked, looked round, and screamed shrilly.

"Murder!" she wailed. "Murder! Police! Fire! Thieves!" She gasped and recovered her breath. "Every penny gone of the money that was to keep the young—."

"What money?" asked the boy. The question seemed to goad Mrs. Rastin to fury.

"Out you go, you little devil," she cried furiously. She took him by the back of his neck.

"Mind my collar," he shouted.

"Out of it," she screamed. "I was goin' to be good-natured enough to keep you whilst the bloomin' money lasted, but now I've had enough of it." She lugged him out, despite his kicks, to the landing. "Now then, out you go."

Bobbie fell down the staircase to the bottom. The commotion had excited the house; doors were open.

"Come in 'ere," said the Duchess kindly. She wore an old, old satin gown, her lean, rope-like throat uncovered. "You come and live long of us. I've of'en wanted a child of me own."

## CHAPTER III

On the Duchess and Mr. Leigh, her husband, leaving Pimlico Walk somewhat hurriedly the next morning with two barrow-loads of furniture and Bobbie Lancaster, Pimlico Walk, led by Mrs. Rastin, did not hesitate to give them verbal testimonials as to character. The husband, Mrs. Rastin suggested, had robbed her of someone else's hard-earned savings; the Duchess was condemned severely by those to whom she had in effusive moments given her confidence. The Duchess's husband was a quiet, resigned-looking man, with a fringe of whiskers that met underneath his chin; his behaviour conveyed the impression that he only desired to be let alone in order that he might do good in a quiet, unobtrusive way. He seemed, in regard to conversation, curt; he never used superfluous words, and before he spoke he always drew in a whistling breath looking around cautiously, as one anxious above all things not to incriminate himself. He for his part took the attacks of the neighbours quite calmly, and when the Duchess, so indignant that she dropped a glass candlestick with lustres, essayed to reply, he begged her to hold her tongue and to come on.

"Least said," remarked the Duchess's husband, "soonest mended. Give us a pound with this barrer."

"And I 'ope," screamed Mrs. Rastin, "that the money'll prove a curse to you if so be that you're the party as took it. What'll become of the poor kid don't bear thinking of."

"You thought you was going to have a 'igh old time," retorted the Duchess, "and you're disappointed. Moment the money was spent you were going to turn the poor boy out neck and crop."

"Don't you measure other ladies by yourself, ma'am," shouted Mrs. Rastin. "You're nothing more nor less than—"

"Come on," said the Duchess's husband.

"But," urged the trembling Duchess, "did you 'ear what she called me?"

"What's it matter?" remarked the man.

Bobbie, helping to push one of the barrows through the Walk, had the happy feeling that he had really been the cause of the disturbance, and that he was engaged in making history very fast. Trixie Bell's mother, standing at the door of her small bonnet shop, shook her head dolefully as she saw him; Bobbie make a grimace at her that checked the excellent woman's sympathy. Behind the shop window Trixie Bell herself looked out between the ostrich-feathered hats with round, astonished eyes.

"What's the number, Leigh?"

Mr. Leigh gave the information as the two barrows turned from Hoxton Street into Ely Place. Ely Place had more breadth than Pimlico Walk, but it was a grim, mysterious thoroughfare, it had none of the shops which served to make Pimlico Walk interesting; certainly a few of the cottages had a plot in front with a slate-coloured lawn, but these were in every case flagged with imperfect drying linen that destroyed any pretence of rusticity. Before one of these the barrows stopped.

A long young woman with sleeves folded back high above her elbow, her red hair in a single knot, swept the step casually with a bald broom.

"'Ullo," she said, "you've arrived, then?"

Mr. Leigh seemed about to reply in the affirmative, but stopped himself leaving the confession to the Duchess.

"Bat's gone out in the Kingsland Road," went on the red-haired young woman.

"What for?" asked the Duchess, unloading the barrows.

"To get change," said the young woman.

This reply amused the Duchess so much that, casting away resentment against the world in general and Pimlico Walk in particular, she rested a chair-bedstead in the dim passage and sat down upon it to enjoy the laugh. Bobbie, anxious to show himself as one of the family, laughed too, and Mr. Leigh almost smiled.

"You are a caution," said the Duchess exhaustedly.

"What 'ave I said now?" asked the young woman, with all a humorist's assumption of gravity.

"It isn't so much what you say as your manner."

"This your tenth?" asked the girl, resting her chin on the broom and nodding her head in the direction of Bobbie.

"He's a little chap," explained the amused Duchess, "that's left without a parent, and we're going to look after him. Ain't we, Leigh?"

"Don't ast me," begged Mr. Leigh.

"He'll come in useful," whispered the Duchess.

"Bat don't care for kids about the place."

"He's as knowing," urged the Duchess, "as a grown-up."

"This is only our town 'ouse," explained the red-haired young woman to Bobbie. "Rather 'andsome, palatial sort of mansion, don't you think?"

"Tell better," said Bobbie, looking round, "when someone's give it a good clean down. What's in the room at the back?"

"You ask my 'usband that question when he comes 'ome," said the young woman with sudden acerbity, "and he'll strap you till he's tired."

"Shan't ask him, then," said Bobbie.

"Never pry, Bobbie," counselled the Duchess warningly. "Little boys that go prying never come to no good. Carry that lamp upright, and don't upset the oil, or I'll upset you."

Bobbie, submitted to Mr. Bat Miller upon that gentleman's return from obtaining change in Kingsland Road, was so fortunate as to obtain favour, and Bat Miller after telling the young woman, who seemed of a jealous disposition, exactly how his time had been occupied, ruffled the boy's head of hair, telling him that if he behaved himself he should learn in that house everything worth knowing. But none of your tricks mind, said Mr. Bat Miller. As a first test Mr. Miller took a bright two shilling-piece from an inside pocket of his waistcoat, and, spite of the protests of the two women, dispatched him with it to a certain shop in Hackney Road to purchase one ounce of shag. When Bobbie returned, panting, with the tobacco in a screw of paper and the change safely in his fist, Bat Miller first tested the coins by trying them with his teeth, and then gave Bobbie for himself a penny, some of the tobacco, and commendation in congratulatory but lurid terms. The two men went out together, and the Duchess and young Mrs. Bat Miller exchanged grievances, Mrs. Miller complaining a good deal of her husband's irregular behaviour, and presently they too, finding themselves in agreement on several questions, went out, locking the boy in that he might look after the house. They promised to be absent for not more than two seconds, but by some error they made it two hours, and during that time Bobbie prowled over the house and went into every room, excepting only the locked-up room at the back of the ground floor.

At the door of this locked-up room he listened very carefully. The keyhole being plugged, he could see nothing, but he kept his ear to the door for some time. It seemed to him that a sound of heavy breathing came from within.

The two couples came home in admirable temper. Even Mr. Leigh's attitude to the world seemed less guarded, and several times he appeared inclined to sing with the rest. They brought in with them fried potatoes, fish, and a large bottle; Bobbie, to his astonishment and great satisfaction, being allowed to help himself. The Duchess repeated the anecdotes of high life in the sixties that Bobbie had heard before, Mr. Leigh watching her with pride as she assumed her accent of refinement, and ordering her to tell more than one account of a past evening twice over. Later, young Mrs. Miller let down her knot of red hair, and recited a touching poem about a Russian mother who being torn from her family to endure punishment in Siberia, apparently objected to it very much and pleaded with the soldiers, but with no avail until presently her youngest born argued with them, and then the officer in charge relenting, kissed the babe and said, "Your mother's safe, my darling child. To you she owes her life; For I, too, have an infant mild, Also a loving wife." At which pleasing point the recital finished, leaving the hearers content, with perhaps a slight fear that the tender-hearted officer might have had some trouble in explaining his conduct to his superior officers. Then Mr. Bat Miller, a little sleepy, sang a long, long song, relating vaguely to the sea, with a refrain of "What ho for the rolling wave, me boys, And a life on the vasty deep," and when he had finished, the Duchess consented, after a good deal of pressing, to give her imitation of a well-known serio-comic lady whose star had been high some twenty-five years previously, a performance requiring a hiccough that the Duchess had no difficulty in repeating. Bobbie had seldom enjoyed an afternoon so much.

"Time for the Fright's 'alf pint, ain't it?" said Mr. Leigh.

The wooden clock on the mantel-piece had just struck twelve, as notification that it was six o'clock.

"Enough left in the jug, ain't there?" asked Mrs. Miller.

"Bit flat."

"He don't care whether its flat or round," said the humorous young woman. "It's all one to the Fright. Bat, wake up and look after your lodger."

Bat Miller awakened, took the large bottle, and went out into the passage.

"Come back, Bobbie," cried the Duchess, sharply. The boy did not obey, being indeed accustomed to persist in doing anything that he was told not to do. Mr. Leigh rushed out, and catching him, swung him back into the room. The two women boxed his ears.

"Stiddy," said the boy resentfully. "Three to one's plenty."

"I've told you before not to pry," said the Duchess.

"Who was prying?"

"Look 'ere," said Mr. Leigh, as peacemaker, "come out 'long o' me."

"Where you goin', Leigh?"

"Station," he said.

"Ain't you reported yourself yet?"

"I ain't," said Mr. Leigh, finding his cap.

"You'll get yourself into trouble some day," remarked the Duchess.

"Wouldn't be the first time," interposed young Mrs. Miller.

"Got the ticket with you?"

"Course I 'ave."

Mr. Leigh took from his inside pocket a sheet of paper about the size of an ordinary letter; he replaced it in an envelope and led Bobbie out of the house. In Kingsland Road they turned to the right. Opposite were the low almshouses standing in their own grounds and protected by a low iron spiked wall. The two went towards Shoreditch.

"Where are we going to book to?" asked Bobbie, "when we get to the station?" Mr. Leigh did not answer. "Going for ride in the train, ain't we?"

"No!"

"What station are we going to, then?"

"Police station."

"'Ere," said the boy, stopping. "None of your 'alf larks.'

"You're all right, kiddy."

"What's the row, then?"

"No row," said Mr. Leigh. "Slight fermality, that's all."

Bobbie's fears proved groundless. Mr. Leigh went up the steps of the police station, where one or two uniformed men and a few men in plain clothes stood under the blue lamp, and these nodded to Mr. Leigh. Bobbie waited in the hall in order that, necessity arising, he might make swift escape, and Mr. Leigh, taking off his cap respectfully, tapped at a wooden window. The window opened; the face of an inspector appeared.

"Evenin', sir," said Mr. Leigh.

"Well, me man?"

"Nice bright, cold autumn weather, sir," said Mr. Leigh, holding his cap between his teeth and finding the sheet of paper. "Soon be 'aving winter on us now."

"I thought it had turned warmer," said the inspector, taking a book down.

"P'raps you're right, sir," said Mr. Leigh obsequiously.

"I ought to remember your name," said the inspector, turning over the pages of the book. "Begins with an L, don't it?"

"You're right again, sir. Name of Leigh—Abraham Leigh."

"I've found it," said the inspector, who had been running his finger down the page. "Got the ticket?"

Mr. Leigh passed in the sheet of letter paper, and the inspector, comparing it with the entry in the book, endorsed it.

"Seems all right," said the inspector.

"Slight alteration of address," remarked Mr. Leigh humbly. "Now residing at 112, Ely Place."

"Rum quarter," said the inspector, as he made a note.

"Must live somewhere, sir," submitted Mr. Leigh.

"Going on straight now?" asked the inspector, as he handed the note back.

"Rather," answered Mr. Leigh complacently. "Turned over a new leaf, I 'ave."

"Good!"

"Other bisness don't pay, sir," said Mr. Leigh, replacing the folded sheet of paper in his pocket. "It's a mug's game, that's what I call it. Good day, sir."

"Good day, me man." Shutting the window to with a decisive snap.

Mr. Leigh, coming down the steps with Bobbie, was spoken to casually by one of the plain clothes men, who in an uninterested way asked Mr. Leigh some questions concerning (it appeared to the boy) mutual acquaintances, but Mr. Leigh seemed unable to give the plain clothes man any of the information desired, complaining as excuse of decaying powers of memory.

"I think it must be I'm getting old, Mr. Thorpe, sir."

"That'll grow on you," said the plain clothes man, "if you aren't careful."

"I can't remember names," declared Mr. Leigh, complainingly; "I can't remember faces; I can't remember any mortal thing."

"Ah," said the detective, "pity!"

To Bobbie, as they walked home to Ely Place, Mr. Leigh appeared slightly more communicative, counselling the boy to behave decorously if ever he should find himself in trouble.

"Inside or outside," declared Mr. Leigh, "it pays in the long run."

At Ely Place everything was in train, the day being special and the evening also out of the ordinary, for a visit to the theatre. Some question arose in regard to the wisdom of leaving the house alone, but young Mrs. Miller said that she wasn't going to be left out of it if Bat were going, the Duchess said it wasn't often she got the chance, Mr. Leigh said he didn't see no particular harm in going to the play, Bat Miller said that too much work told on a man; that the Fright would be safe enough, and it would make a nice change for all of them. So they all went. Bat Miller locked the door with great care, and in five minutes they were finding their way up the broad stone stairs of the Britannia with a struggling, anxious, noisy, good-tempered crowd.

"Right sort," suggested Mr. Leigh, in a whisper to Bat Miller, as they forced their way to the pay box.

"I'm sure," agreed Bat Miller. "Don't want no fuss 'ere." He pinched the ear of a dark young woman in front of him.

"I'll have your black eyes," he said admiringly.

"You'll get two of your own if you ain't careful," retorted the girl, not displeased.

"Shouldn't mind being punched by you," said Bat Miller. "Let me keep these others from scrouging you."

"Bat," cried a voice behind him.

"Now begin agin."

"Leave off talkin' to that nigger gel," commanded young Mrs. Miller.

"Who are you callin' a nigger gel," inquired the dark young woman across the heads of the surging crowd, "carrots?"

"You," replied Mrs. Miller frankly, "Miss Tar Brush."

"Don't answer her," begged Mr. Bat Miller to his new acquaintance. "She's so jealous she can't see straight."

"I pity you," said the dark young woman.

"So do I," said Mr. Miller softly. "Lemme get your ticket for you."

A roaring noisy crowded gallery, like the side of a mountain going from the base with strong iron rods protecting up to the topmost point, where patrons had to bend their backs to escape the ceiling. General discardment of coats by men and boys, universal doffing of hats and bonnets, and loosening of blouses by ladies. Bobbie, perched on the rolled-up coats of the two men, saw at a distance of what seemed at first to be several miles below, the tightly-wedged people on the floor of the theatre packed closely to the very footlights, and leaving just sufficient room for a small orchestra. Mrs. Bat Miller, still trembling with annoyance, bought oranges, and selecting one over ripe, stood up and threw it, and more by luck than skill, managed to hit the dark young woman, seated below, well on the side of the face, where it burst shell-like and caused annoyance. Having done this, young Mrs. Miller seemed more content, and twisting up her rope of red hair, settled down to unrestrained enjoyment of the evening.

"I wouldn't 'ave your dispisition," said Mr. Bat Miller to her, wistfully, "for a bloomin' pension."

Bobbie felt pleased to see the two boys from Drysdale Street far above him; they would require all the austerity that a railway arch could give to prevent them from feeling envious of him. He held up a piece of apple and shouted above the babel of voices, "'Ave 'alf?" and when they screamed back "Yus!" he ate it all calmly; thus goading them to a state of speechless vexation. Everybody called to everybody else; the enormous theatre filled with appeals for recognition. Presently through the uproar could be heard the discordant tuning up of the violins, and, holding the Duchess's thin arm, he looked down again and saw that the orchestra had come in.

The footlights being turned up, the violins began to play. The Duchess said it was nothing to the Alhambra in the old days, but Bobbie felt this could not be true. When the curtain ascended and the uniformed men posted in various quarters of the large theatre bawled for silence, Bobbie held tightly to the Duchess for fear that he might be tempted to jump over.

It was not easy to discover at first the true intent of the play, because the gallery did not at once become quiet; two fights and a faint were necessary before quietude could be obtained. When the words from the far-off stage came up more distinctly to Bobbie's quick ears, he realized that a plot was being arranged by two gentlemanly men in evening dress to rob the bank of the sum of fifty thousand pounds, and it seemed that they wished to do this unobtrusively, and indeed desired that any credit for its success should be placed to the account not of themselves, but of the manager of the bank. The manager came on just then to a majestic air from the orchestra; the audience seemed to know him, for they cheered, and he stood in the centre of the stage bowing condescendingly before he commenced to interest himself in the drama. He was rather a noble-looking young man, a little stout perhaps, with a decided way of speaking; you could hear every word he said, and when he had to make any movement the orchestra played briskly, as though to intimate that whatever misfortune might cross his path, he had always the support of four fiddlers, two bass viols, a cornet, a pianist, and a trombone. The two villains intimated their desire to open an account at the bank. The manager asked for references. The two villains, first looking cautiously off at the wings to make sure that no one observed them, suddenly flung themselves on the bank manager. They were engaged in binding him with ropes, when a ragged boy (who the Duchess said was not a boy but a girl) jumped in at the window, and said,—

"What price me!"

Upon which the two villains instantly decamped; the ragged boy summoned the clerks (who, reasonably speaking, should have heard the struggle, but apparently did not), and the manager ordered that the ragged boy should he offered a highly responsible post in the bank, for, said the manager to the gallery, of what use is sterling honesty in this world if it be not liberally rewarded? a sentiment with which the gallery found itself able to express cordial agreement. In the next scene the two gentlemanly villains, undeterred by their rebuff, were seen in a vague light, drilling with caution the cardboard door of an immense safe of the bank. They had but just succeeded when voices were heard. Plaintive music and entrance of heroine. Dressed in white, she had come to bring a posy of flowers to the manager, whom, it appeared, she was to marry on the morrow. This visit seemed unnecessary, and it was certainly indiscreet; after the manager had surprised her and had given to the gallery a few choice opinions on the eternal power of Love, which made Mrs. Bat Miller so agitated that her rope of red hair became untied, the heroine went, after an affectionate farewell, leaving a note on the floor.

"You've dropped something, Miss," shouted Bobbie.

"'Ush," warned the Duchess. "That's done a purpose."

This note the villains found, after a struggle with the girl boy, who, demanding of them, "What price me?" was clubbed on the head, and left insensible. The note only required a slight alteration with the tearing off of one page to be construed into evidence of complicity in the crime; so that when, in the next scene, a cheerful wedding party in secondhand clothes came out of the church door, bells ringing, villagers strewing flowers, and wedding march from the orchestra, two constables suddenly pushed their way through the crowd and placed hands on the shoulders of the astonished bride, causing so much consternation that the bells stopped, the wedding march changed into a hurried frantic movement, what time the bride clutched at her bodice, and assured the gallery (but this they knew full well) that she was innocent. A boy inspector, with a piping voice, stepped forward and proceeded to act in accordance with stage law. Woman, I arrest you. Oh, sir, explain. This letter (said the inspector) in your handwriting was found in the bank after the robbery. Sir, said the tearful bride, 'tis true I wrote that letter, but—. Woman (said the stern boy inspector), prevarication is useless; who were your accomplices? You decline to answer? Good! Officers, do your duty. Scoundrels (shouted the bridegroom bank manager), unhand her, before God she is innocent as the driven snow, I swear it. Ho, ho (remarked the boy inspector, acutely putting two and two together), then this can only mean—here the orchestra became quite hysterical—that you yourself are guilty. Officers, arrest him also! May Heaven, begged the bride emotionally, addressing the gallery, may Heaven in its great mercy, protect the innocent and the pure. It seemed that Heaven proved somewhat tardy in responding to the heroine's appeal, for from a quarter to eight until a quarter to eleven, she and the hero found themselves in a succession of the direst straits, which, apportioned with justice, would have been more than enough for fifty young couples. It did seem that they could not by any dexterity do the right thing; whereas, the two villains, on the contrary, prospered exceedingly, to the special annoyance of Mr. Bat Miller, who, constituting himself leader of a kind of vigilance committee in the hot perspiring gallery, led off the hisses whenever either or both appeared, and at certain moments—as, for instance, when in the hospital ward they lighted their cigarettes, and discussed cynically the prospect of the injured boy's speedy departure from life—hurling down at them appropriate and forcible words of reproof, that did credit alike to his invention and to the honesty of his feelings.

It is only fair to add that the gallery gave to Mr. Miller ready and unanimous assistance. How they yelled with delight when the boy (who was a girl) defied one of the villains, and bade him do his worst! How they shivered when the villain, producing a steel dagger, crept furtively up to the boy, whose back was turned, and how they shouted with rapture as the boy, swinging round at exactly the right moment, presented a revolver at the villain's forehead, causing that despicable person to drop the dagger and go weak at the knees. How they held their breath when, on the boy incautiously laying down the revolver and going to look at the wings, the villain obtained possession of the deadly weapon, and covered the boy with it. And then when the boy had affected to cower and to beg for mercy (which, it need hardly be said, the villain flatly declined to grant), how they screamed with mad ecstasy on the boy saying with sudden calm,—

"By-the-bye! Hadn't you better make sure that that little pop-gun's loaded?"

Causing the villain to curse his fate and to snap the trigger ineffectually, thus giving the boy a cue for saying once more,—

"What price me!"

Bobbie in support whistled and hissed and howled so much, that after a while he became exhausted, and to his regret found himself unable to express opinions with vigour; this did not, however, prevent him from weeping bitter tears over the hospital scene. It was in the hospital scene, as a matter of fact, that the luck of the hero and heroine turned. The injured youngster suddenly recovered sight and reason; denounced the two villains, now cringing beneath the triumphant, hysterical theatre; called upon the boy inspector, fortunately at the wings, to arrest them, which the boy inspector instantly did, thus retrieving his position in the esteem of the audience; amid an increasing hum of approval from the mountain of heads in front, the youngster arranged from his couch for the future happiness of the hero and heroine, capping it all and extracting a roar from the house by remarking,—

"Now, what price me!"

Which might have been the pure essence distilled from all the best jokes of all time, judging from its instantaneous and admirable effect. Then the hero and heroine, at the centre of the stage, managed to intimate that sunshine had broken through the clouds; that trustful and loving, they would now proceed to live a life of absolute peace and perfect happiness; the orchestra feeling itself rewarded at last for all its faithful attention, broke out into a triumphant march, and—rideau.

In Hoxton Street it was drizzling, and the crowd surging out of the doorway turned up its coat collars and tied handkerchiefs over its bonnets, and set off for home. Bobbie, dazed with excitement, clutched the Duchess's yellow skirt and trotted along, after a minute's rest at a whelk stall, the two men and Mrs. Miller following closely behind. At the corner of Essex Street they waited to allow a four-wheeler to go by. The elderly horse, checked by the driver, slipped, and nearly fell, recovered itself, and slipped again, made vain efforts to get a secure footing, and upon the driver standing up to use his whip and saying bitterly, "Why don't you fall down and 'ave done with it," did fall down, and remained there. A small crowd formed without a moment's delay; Mr. Bat Miller went to the stout old gentleman inside the cab, now trying without success to let down the window, and opening the door, assured him with great courtesy that he had no cause for fear. Having done this, Mr. Miller re-closed the door and stepped back. He passed something furtively to red-haired Mrs. Miller, who slipped the something into Bobbie's pocket, telling him in a commanding whisper to cut off home like mad. Bobbie, feeling that he was helping in some proceeding of an imperial nature, complied, noting as he darted away the very stout gentleman hammering with his fists at the closed window of the four-wheeler. Mr. Miller sauntered off Kingsland Road way; the two women and Mr. Leigh went unconcernedly to a public-house.

Bobbie was shivering when five minutes later the company rejoined him at the street door of the house in Ely Place. Mr. Miller found his key and let them in. The smelly lamp in the passage burned low; in the closed back room a quavering voice sang a hymn.

"Dare to be a Daniyul,
Dare to stand alone,
Dare to 'ave a purpose firm,
And dare—"

"Shut it!" commanded Bat Miller, knocking at the door of the back room sharply. "Get off to sleep, can't you?" He turned to the others. "And now," he said with a change of manner, "let's see what kind of a little present this young genelman's bin and brought 'ome for us."

"I b'lieve he pinched it for me," said young Mrs. Miller cheerfully, "'cause to-day isn't my birthday."

Bobbie, with something of majesty, brought from his pocket a heavy gold watch and part of a gold chain, and laid them on the table. The four put their heads together and examined the property. Then they beamed round upon the small boy.

"I foresee, Bobbie," said the Duchess, in complimentary tones, "that you're a goin' to grow up a bright, smart, useful young chep."

"He'll want trainin'," suggested Mr. Bat Miller.

"And watchin'," growled Mr. Leigh.

"And when he gets to be a man," said young Mrs. Miller facetiously, as she pulled off her boots, "all the gels in the neighbourhood 'll be after him."

With these praises clanging and resounding in his heated little brain, Bobbie went upstairs to bed.


CHAPTER IV

For nearly a year Bobbie Lancaster lived his young life in Ely Place. Although every day was not so full of incident as the first, he could not charge dulness against his existence; the standard of happiness set up in Ely Place not being a high one, was therefore easily reached; monotony at any rate came rarely. When other plans failed, quarrels could always be relied upon, and these gave such joy, not only to the chief actors and actresses, but also to the audience, that it seemed small wonder so successful a performance should be frequently repeated. Now and again events occurred which flattered Bobbie, and gave him the dearest satisfaction a small boy can experience—that of being treated as though he were grown up. It had not taken Mr. Leigh and Mr. Bat Miller long to recognize that in Bobbie they had a promising apprentice; one so obstinately honest as to be of great assistance to them in their dishonest profession. They exercised due caution in taking him into their confidence. For instance, he was still at the end of the year not sure why it was that the back room on the ground floor remained always locked; why its windows, facing a yard, and overlooked by the huge straggling workhouse, were closely shuttered. He knew that a man worked there; he knew that this man was called The Fright, and Mrs. Miller, on one expansive evening when in admirable humour, told him that The Fright was by trade a silver chaser. Presuming on some additional knowledge acquired at a time when supposed to be asleep, he demanded of the two men further particulars; Mr. Bat Miller replied fiercely that spare the rod and spoil the child had never been his motto, and thereupon gave Bobbie the worst thrashing that the boy had ever dreamed of. Following this, the boy found himself for some days treated with great coldness by the adult members of the household, and made to feel that he was no longer in the movement. When either of the men went out in the evening, the boy was not permitted to go also; he found himself deprived of adventurous excursions into the suburbs; the casual loafing about at busy railway stations was denied to him. So keenly did he feel this ostracism that he had tumultuous thoughts of giving himself up to the School Board inspector whom he had hitherto dodged, and of devoting his time to the acquirement of useful knowledge; it is right to add that the idea of betraying any of the secrets which he had learnt concerning the habits of the two men never for a moment occurred to him. An alternative was to buy a revolver similar to the one possessed by Teddy Sullivan, and to go out somewhere and shoot someone; the latter faintly-sketched plan was rubbed out because Master Sullivan, his friend, encountered disaster one evening in Union Street. In the course of a strenuous hand-to-hand fight between Hackney Road boys and Hoxton boys, a point arrived where the Hoxton boys found themselves badly worsted, whereupon Master Sullivan, with a sentence plagiarized from a penny romance which he knew almost by heart, "Ten thousand furies take you, you dastardly scoundrels," whipped out his revolver, and closing his eyes, fired, injuring two or three promising juveniles from the tributary streets of Hackney Road, and, as a last consequence of this act, finding himself exposed to the glory of police court proceedings, and to the indignity of a birching.

Tension was snapped by a quarrel between Mr. Bat Miller and his young wife. There were times when Mrs. Bat Miller was obtrusively affectionate with her husband; as compensation, occasions flew in when she became half mad with jealousy. The Duchess and Mr. Leigh at these crises acted as peacemakers, a task at times not easy; in this particular case they failed entirely. The young woman tore her red hair with fury; she screamed so loudly that, common as such exhibitions were in Ely Place, neighbours began to show some interest in the front door. In this difficulty Mr. Bat Miller, pained and distressed, appealed to Bobbie to state whether so far from having been walking with the sister of Nose, the boy of Drysdale Street, between the hours of nine and ten that evening, he had not as a matter of fact been in the company of Bobbie at Liverpool Street Station. To this question Bobbie (who at the hours mentioned had been having a gloomy and quite solitary game of hop-scotch at the Kingsland Road end of Ely Place) answered promptly, "Yus!" and Mrs. Bat Miller confronted with this proof of alibi burst into regretful tears and reproached herself for a silly woman, one who allowed herself to be taken in by the gossip of any spiteful cat of a neighbour. Mr. Miller, grateful to Bobbie for this timely assistance, persuaded the quiet Leigh to allow the boy to resume his position in their confidence. After some hesitation Mr. Leigh agreed, adding, however, that he hoped Bobbie would see that the first duty of little boys was to be seen and not heard; the second, not to go about interfering with what did not concern them. These Mr. Leigh declared to be ever golden rules, not to be broken without danger. Bobbie promised to bear the advice carefully in mind, and re-assumed his position in the house with satisfaction.

The two women were nearly always kind to him, and to them he became indebted for cheerful hours. The proudest memory of the Duchess's was that of her one appearance on the music hall stage. It seemed that another young lady and herself, having, in the late sixties, saved their money, had made their bow from the small stage of a small hall attached to a small public-house in Banner Street, St. Luke's. They called themselves the Sisters Montmorency (on the urgent recommendation of the agent), and sang a song which still remained her favourite air. When in very good temper and when Bobbie had been a very good boy, she would go out of the room, and re-enter with a fine swish of the skirts singing in a thin, quavering voice this verse:—

You should see us in our landor when we're drivin' in the Row,
You should 'ear us chaff the dukes and belted earls;
We're daughters of nobility, so they treat us with ceevility,
For of well-bred, high-class damsels we're the pearls.

It appeared that the two débutantes quarrelled with each other after the first performance over some point of etiquette and fought in Banner Street, St. Luke's; as a consequence the partnership had thereupon been dissolved, and the Duchess's career as an artiste of the music halls found itself checked and stopped.

Proud in the ownership of a new bowler hat; magnificent in the possession of a four-bladed knife with a corkscrew, which had come to him as his share of the contents of a portmanteau labelled from Scarborough to King's Cross, and taken possession of at the latter station by Mr. Miller before the owner had time to claim it, Bobbie strolled along Old Street one evening, smoking a cigarette, and pushing small girls off the pavement into the roadway. Behind him walked Miss Trixie Bell, feathered hatted and a skirt furtively let out after departure from her mother's shop in Pimlico Walk; Miss Bell, in crossing lakes on the pavement, felt justified in lifting her skirt carefully to avoid contact with the ground, which it cleared by about twelve inches. At a junction of the City Road the boy stopped to allow the confused trams to untie themselves, and looking round saw her.

"Cheer!" said Miss Bell with defiant shyness. "How's the world using you?" Bobbie did not answer. "You ain't seen me for a long time."

"Ain't wanted," replied the boy.

"I've been away in the country," said the young woman, in no way disconcerted. "'Mongst medders and pigs and farm yards and nuts, and I don't know what all."

"Well," he said, "what of it?"

"You still living in Ely Place?"

"P'raps I am; p'raps I ain't."

"I wouldn't live there for something," remarked the girl, shrugging her shoulders.

"They wouldn't let you," replied the boy. "They're very particular about the kerricter of people they 'ave there."

"Must they all 'ave a bad kerricter?" asked Miss Bell innocently.

The trams at the junction of roads extricated themselves from the tangle, and people who had been waiting on the kerb went across the roadway. Trixie Bell followed Bobbie, and they walked on opposite sides of the dimly-lighted pavement near St. Luke's Asylum, continuing their conversation with breaks occasioned by intervening passers-by.

"You've no call," shouted the boy, "to come follering me about. I don't want no truck with gels."

"I s'pose you've bought the street, ain't you?" asked Miss Bell loudly. "Seem to think you're everybody 'cause you've got a bowler 'at on. Be wearing a chimney-pot next, I lay."

"Shan't ask your permission."

"All the boys down in the country," called out the girl, "wash 'emselves twice a day."

"More fools them," said Bobbie.

"They wouldn't dare be seen going about with a dirty face and neck like what you've got."

"Look 'ere," said the boy savagely. He moved nearer to her. "You leave my face and neck alone."

"Sorry to do otherwise," she remarked pertly.

"When I want any remarks from you 'bout my face and neck I'll ast for 'em. Till then you keep your mouth shut 'r I'll shut it for you."

"You'd do a lot."

Bobbie lifted his arm, but the small girl did not flinch. He made another threatening gesture; instantly his new bowler hat went spinning into the middle of the road in imminent danger of being run over by a railway van. Bobbie rescued it adroitly, and returning chased Miss Bell as far as Goswell Road.

"Don't hit me," she begged, panting; "I won't do it again."

"Time's come," said the boy hotly, "when I've got to punch your bloomin' 'ead for you."

"Lemme off this time," craved Miss Bell, crouching against a shop window, "and I'll stand you a ride back by tram."

"You ain't got no tuppence," said Bobbie, relenting.

"I've got thruppence," she said.

They walked on as far as Bloomsbury in order that they might have full money's worth. When they boarded a departing tram, and the conductor shouted to them to get off, it delighted Bobbie very much to be able to confound the man by declaring themselves as passengers. To do honour to the occasion the boy rolled a cigarette, and, turning to a tall spectacled young man on the seat behind them, borrowed a match.

"Take two," said the tall young man.

As the tram sailed past the lighted shops in Theobald's Road, Trixie passed the twopence furtively to her companion, who paid the conductor with a lordly air, offering at the same time a few criticisms on the conductor's appearance. Presently the girl touched very lightly his hand and moved nearer to him.

"Keep your 'ead off my shoulder," he remarked brusquely.

"I want to tell you something," said Trixie.

"Needn't get so close."

"My mother says—"

"What," said Bobbie, "is the old cat still alive?"

"My mother says that if you like to leave those people what you're with now and come and work at our shop as a errand boy—"

"A errand boy," echoed Bobbie amazedly. "Work at that bloomin' 'ole in the wall?'

"She'll give you eighteen-pence a week and see that you 'ave good schooling, and arrange so that you grow up respectable."

Bobbie, recovering from his astonishment, placed his cigarette on the seat in order that he might laugh without restraint.

"Of all the dam bits of cheek!" he declared exhaustedly.

"Make a lot of difference to you," said the wise young woman. "If you don't grow up respectable you'll simply—"

"Me, respectable," said the amused boy. "Why, you silly little ijiot, d'you think I don't know a trick worth fifty of that. I ain't going to work for my bloomin' livin'."

"Won't 'ave a chance to if the police get 'old of you."

"Is that another one of your Mar's remarks? 'Cause, if so, you tell her from me, that she's a—"

"Let's get down 'ere," said Trixie Bell. She interrupted the string of adjectives by rising; there were tears in her eyes. "This is 'Oxton Street."

"You can," said the boy. "I'm goin' on to Shoreditch."

"Wish I—I hadn't met you now," she said, with a catch in her voice.

"Don't let it 'appen again."

"I'll never speak to you," sobbed Trixie Bell, "never no more in all my life."

"Best bit of news I've 'eard for a age."

"Don't you expect—don't you expect me ever to take notice of you in future, mind."

"If you do," said Bobbie, "I shall be under the pineful necessity of knocking your 'ead clean off."

"Goo'-bye," said the girl hesitatingly.

"Be slippy," said Bobbie.

The tall young man on the seat behind leaned forward as Trixie Bell disappeared down the steps of the tram. He tapped Bobbie on the shoulder.

"You behaved rather discourteously, sir, to your fair companion," he said.

"Go on!" said Bobbie, recklessly. "All of you manage my affairs! Don't mind me! I'll sit back and not do nothing."

"My excuse must be that we have met before. My name is Myddleton West, and I was at an inquest once—"

"I remember," said the boy.

"Is the lady who has just gone engaged to you, may I ask?"

"No fear," said Bobbie, disdainfully. "She's a bit gone on me, that's all. Perfect nuisance it is, if you ask me."

"This," said Myddleton West, "shows how awkward Providence is. With some of us the case is exactly the reverse."

"You're a lump better off without 'em," said the boy sagely.

"I only want one."

"And one," said Bobbie, "is sometimes one too many. What are you doing in this quarter? Thought you lived 'Olborn way."

"I want the police station in Kingsland Road," said the journalist. "I have to see the inspector about something. Do you know it?"

"Do I not?" said Bobbie confidently.

They descended at the turbulent junction of roads near Shoreditch Station, and the boy conducted Myddleton West along the noisy crowded pavement of Kingsland Road, under the railway arch towards the police station. Glancing down Drysdale Street as he passed, Bobbie noticed Bat Miller near the gas-lamp talking to Nose's sister; observed also in the shadow of the arch Mrs. Bat Miller watching the scene, her face white and her lips moving. As soon as he had shown Myddleton West the entrance to the police station, and had received sixpence for his pains, he hurried through to Hoxton Street, coming back into Drysdale Street from that end. His intention had been to witness the comedy that he assumed to be impending; to his great regret, just as Mr. Bat Miller began to punch the dark young woman affectionately, the young men who guarded Drysdale Street from the ruthless invader suddenly appeared, led by Nose and by Libbis, and the odds being about eight to one, drove him off with furious threats. He went back to the police station in order to complete the earning of his sixpence by reconducting Myddleton West to the tram for Bloomsbury. Approaching the station, on the steps of which plain clothes men were as usual lounging, he saw Mrs. Bat Miller on the opposite side of the roadway, her white apron over her head, beckoning to one of the plain clothes men. Then she walked carelessly into Union Street. The detective followed her. Bobbie slipped across and stood in a doorway.

"Well, my dear," said the detective. "What's your little game?"

"Mr. Thorpe," said Mrs. Bat Miller, panting. She pressed one hand against her bodice and gasped for breath. "Do you want—want to do a fair cop?"

"A fair cop," said Mr. Thorpe, cheerfully, "would just now come in very handy. Who are the parties?"

"He's behaved like a wretch," said the young woman breathlessly, "or I'd never 'are turned on him. I'm as striteforward a gel as ever breathed in all 'Oxton, ain't I, Mr. Thorpe?"

"No one more so," agreed the detective. "What's the name of—"

"Anything else I could 'ave forgive him," she said, trembling with passion. "When we've been 'ard up and he's come 'ome with not a penny in his pocket and me gone without dinner, did I complain?"

"Course you didn't. Who—"

"When he was put away for six months three year ago, didn't I slave and keep myself to myself, and go and meet him down at Wandsworth when he came out?"

"No lady," conceded Mr. Thorpe, "could have done more. What is—"

"When he was laid up in the orsepital," she went on fiercely, "didn't I go to see him every visiting day and take him nuts and oranges and goodness knows what all, and sit be his bedside for the hour together?"

"I really don't know," said the detective impartially, "what men are coming to. Where are—"

"And then to go paying his attentions to a—"

"Not so loud!"

She checked herself and looked round. Then she took the lapel of Mr. Thorpe's coat and whispered. Bobbie could not hear the words.

"Good!" exclaimed the detective. "Are they both indoors now?"

"If they ain't you can wait for 'em," she replied.

"Will six men be enough d'you think?"

"Six 'll be ample, Mr. Thorpe," she said. "And if Miller shows fight, tell them not to be afraid of knocking him about. It'll do him good, the—"

"I'll make a note of it," said Mr. Thorpe. "You don't want to come with us, I s'pose? You'd better not be seen p'raps?"

"You leave me to look after meself," she answered.

"Come over and 'ave a cup of tea along with our female searcher," suggested Mr. Thorpe.

"Tea be 'anged," she said. "I shall want something stronger than tea when my paddy's over."

"Daresay we shall be able to get you a sovereign or two for this job if you keep yourself quiet."

"Keep your money," she cried angrily. "All I want is to be at the Sessions when he comes up and to watch her face."

Bobbie crept from his doorway. Once in Kingsland Road, he flew along swiftly, slipping in and out of the crowd, and jumping a linen basket, to the astonishment of the two women who were carrying it. He scuttled through the dwarf posts and down Ely Place, knocking over one or two children toddling about in the way, and reaching the house so exhausted that he could only just give the usual whistle at the key-hole. Mr. Leigh opened the door, and seeing him took off the chain. The boy, staggering into the dimly-lighted passage leaned against the wall.

"Bat Miller in?" he panted.

"What's the row?" demanded Mr. Leigh concernedly. Bobbie explained in a hurried, detached, spasmodic way. Mr. Leigh took a pair of scissors from his pocket, and, glancing at a slip of looking-glass, cut off the whiskers which fringed his face.

"Tell the wife," said Mr. Leigh, quietly snipping, "to meet me at Brenchley, if she gets clear. Tell her not to make no fuss." He took his overcoat from the peg, and a cloth cap with ear flaps. "Come straight here 'ave you?" he asked.

"Like a bloomin' arrer."

"Look outside and see if they've come up yet," requested Mr. Leigh, tying the flaps of his cap under his chin. "We don't want no bother or nothing."

Ely Place being clear at the Hoxton Street end, Mr. Leigh, his head well down, went out of the doorway. He shook hands with Bobbie.

"You're a capital boy," whispered Mr. Leigh, approvingly. "If I'd got anything smaller than a tanner about me I'd give it you. Be good!"

Bobbie closed the door, and his heart fluttering, went upstairs to the front bedroom. The Duchess was asleep, dressed, on her bed; her high-heeled boots ludicrously obtrusive. Bobbie aroused her and gave her the news.

"My old man's safe, then? What about Bat Miller?" she asked, sitting up, affrightedly.

"We must watch out of the winder," ordered Bobbie. "If he comes first we'll wave him to be off; if he comes after they're 'ere he'll be nabbed."

"You've got a 'ead on you," said the Duchess, trembling, "that would be a credit to a Prime Minister. Come to the winder and—Let me 'old your 'and, I'm all of a shake."

"They can't touch us, can they?" asked Bobbie, stroking the woman's thin trembling wrist.

"Hope not," said the Duchess, nervously. "But there, you never know what the law can do. Fancy her turning nark jest through a fit of jealousy. Is that Miller talking to one of the neighbours?"

Mr. Miller it was. Mr. Miller, chatting amiably with one of the lady neighbours on the subject of flowers and how to rear them; the lady neighbour being something of a horticulturist in her way, possessing, as she did, in her garden plot, one sooty shrub, a limp sunflower, and several dandelions. Mr. Miller had just said something to the lady neighbour which had made her laugh uproariously, when, chancing to look up, he saw the signals of the Duchess and of Bobbie. His face took a note of interrogation; they motioned to him to go away with all despatch. Mr. Bat Miller crammed his hat over his head and ran off blindly; so blindly indeed that, at the Kingsland Road end of the place, he jumped into the arms of three overcoated men led by Mr. Thorpe; escaping these, he was caught neatly by uniformed policemen who were close behind. At the same moment a similar force appeared at the Hoxton Street end of the place. Bobbie and the Duchess held each other's hands and went downstairs. The faint sound of a hymn came from the closed door.

Three loud raps at the front door. Bobbie went along the passage and opened it. Mr. Thorpe, with the other men; out in the court a small interested crowd, the noise of windows being thrown up.

"Come about the white-washin'?" asked Bobbie, innocently.

"Take the chain off, me lad," said Mr. Thorpe, with his foot inside.

"Right you are, sir."

The men came into the dark passage and one of them flashed a bull's-eye lantern around.

"Father in?" asked Mr. Thorpe.

"Well, no," answered the boy, "he isn't exactly in, sir."

"Won't be long, I daresay."

"I wouldn't wait, sir," said Bobbie respectfully, "if I was you. Fact is he's been dead some years."

The man with the bull's-eye made the circle of light dance to the bottom stair and discovered the Duchess. Another went to the closed door of the back room and put his shoulder against it.

"Now then, ma'am," said Mr. Thorpe, turning from the boy impatiently. "Where's your good gentleman?"

"Pray don't ask me, fellow," replied the Duchess, endeavouring to assume her accent of refinement with some want of success. "If you want him, I really think the best thing you can do is to find him."

"Go upstairs, two of you," commanded Mr. Thorpe. "Two others give Baker a help with that door. Someone look after this woman and the kid."

Bobbie, his shoulder gripped by a broad hand, watched with interest. The door groaned complainingly for a moment or two; then it gave way with so much suddenness that the two men stumbled into the room. Between the figures of the men Bobbie could see the room crowded in the manner of a workshop of limited accommodation. A wooden bench stood against the shuttered windows; the flare of a fire out of sight reddened the untidy floor. On a table some circular moulds of plaster of Paris; near, some coins with a tail of metal attached that gave them an unconvincing appearance. Three pewter pots, half melted on the edge of an iron sink. A small battery in the corner, and at this seated the figure of a young man. The figure looked round casually as' the men entered, and Bobbie caught sight of a face not pleasant to look upon.

"Is that the Fright?" whispered Bobbie to the Duchess. The Duchess nodded and touched her forehead.

"Tile loose!" she said.

The figure turned back to his work of plating, crooning his hymn as though the interruption was not worthy of any special notice. Then the door partially closed.

"Mind my shoulder, please," said the Duchess affectedly.

"I am minding it," said the detective cheerfully.

"You're no gentleman," declared the Duchess, "or you wouldn't behave to a lady in this way."

"I was never what you may call a society man," said the detective. "You seem to have got a rare old little snide factory here all to yourself."

"I beg your pardon!" said the Duchess icily.

"Carried on nice and quiet too, apparently. No show, no display, no what you may call arrogance about it."

"What is this person talking about, Bobbie, my dear?"

"Ast him," said Bobbie, his eyes fixed on the partially-closed door.

"This your boy, ma'am?"

"Are you addressing your conversation to me, sir?"

"Who does the kid belong to?"

"This lad," said the Duchess, precisely, "is, I regret to say, an orphan. I took some interest in his case, and my husband and myself have, so to speak, adopted him."

"Then you'll probably have to unadopt him," said the detective. "If he's got no relatives the State will take him in hand."

"Who's she?" asked Bobbie, detaching his interest from the back room.

"The State's got a pretty decent-sized family as it is," went on the man, "and one extra won't make much difference." His two colleagues came downstairs. "Anybody?" he asked. The two men replied not a soul.

"Then one of 'em's nipped off," said the detective. "Go and tell the sergeant."

The door re-opened as the men proceeded to obey. Between two of Mr. Thorpe's assistants came the demented man, his terrible face down; Bobbie was pulled back to allow them to conduct him through the passage. Finding himself going at a regular pace, he commenced to sing huskily a Moody and Sankey hymn with a marching rhythm.

"Hold the gospel banner high,
On to victory grand,
Satan and his hosts defy,
And shout for Danyul's band."

"Bring the woman and the boy," ordered Mr. Thorpe. "And keep close round them. There's an awkward crowd outside."

The awkward crowd of Ely Place was not apparently ready to carry its awkwardness to the point of interference with the police. On the contrary, the crowd seemed anxious to show some friendliness towards the plain clothes men, saying, Good evening, Mr. Thorpe, sir; more work for you, I see. And how are you, Mr. Baker? and how's that cold of yours getting on, I wonder? Some of the men of Mr. Thorpe's regiment remained in charge of the house; the others assisted in conducting the three arrested people to the police station.

"Hullo, young man," said Myddleton West, at the entrance. The crowd in Kingsland Road had swelled to the number of hundreds, and West had to wait for their departure. "You in this affair?"

"Looks like it," said Bobbie.

"Can I do anything?" asked the long young journalist.

"Yes!"

"Tell me!"

"Keep your head shut," said the boy gruffly. "I don't want no one interfering with my affairs."

"Deplorable thing," remarked Myddleton West aside to the sergeant, "for a child like that."

"Not at all, sir," said Mr. Thorpe, "not at all. We've nabbed him just in time."


CHAPTER V

Events occurred with a rapidity that, in view of their importance, seemed to Bobbie frankly indecorous. No sooner had he been placed between parallel iron bars in a police court than he was whisked from the iron bars, on the direction of a magistrate, who had a kindly manner with children; after a brief week at the workhouse, looked after by a burly inmate (known to colleagues by the satirical name of the Slogger), Bobbie found himself again carried off swiftly to the court, where, when a number of cases had been heard in which foreign gentlemen and foreign ladies told everything but the truth, Bobbie was hurried in and directed to stand by the side of the dock, an order that annoyed him because this was clearly an attempt to treat him as though he were not a grown up and a perfect criminal. In the rooms adjoining the court he had seen Bat Miller, and Bat Miller had had opportunity of mentioning that he was the only one who would get put away, and that when he came out it would be his pleasurable duty to see that Mrs. Bat Miller found herself repaid for all her trouble.

Scarce had the boy taken up an attitude of "don't care" at the side of the dock, and scarce had he commenced to prepare a short remark of defiance for the benefit of Master Ted Sullivan, the shooting youth (whom he saw at the back of the court), when he found himself hustled out of the court by the public door; on kicking the gaoler protestingly in leaving, the gaoler boxed his ears, telling him that he would find somebody outside to teach him manners. Outside, indeed, was an official from the workhouse, who re-conducted him to the huge building that threw out its wings in various directions at the back of Ely Place, and there they had no sooner arrived than Bobbie, being now the charge and ward of the guardians, found himself added to a party of children made up of six boys and seven girls (nearly all of them younger than himself), who were carried away in charge of the Slogger and a grim, silent comrade of the Slogger, to a London station that Bobbie knew, there to take train for the parish schools which Wisdom, looking in some years before at a meeting of the Guardians, had suggested. All this rapidity of action made the boy extremely sulky; when the Slogger, in workhouse uniform, offered him a few choice flowers of advice culled from the spacious gardens of experience, in the shape of hints on the way of living in the world at the minimum of labour to yourself and the maximum of expense to other people, Bobbie growled at the Slogger's well-meant counsel, and would have found the journey away into Essex tedious but for the fact that he heard a woman in the next compartment remark that he possessed a bright little face. The compliment saved him from depression, and made him put his cap straight.

Arrived at a country station, the small band of thin-faced children marched out into the roadway in charge of the two men. One of the youngest baby girls had just decided the moment to be opportune for wailing, when they happened on a scene that changed the attitude of everybody from the Slogger down to the smallest boy in petticoats. The sight being new to Bobbie, his interest and delight increased accordingly. The Slogger seemed to have exercised enough energy at some period of his life to have obtained certain information, and was in consequence able to give the scene a title.

"A cirkiss!" said the Slogger authoritatively.

A circus it was! Not one of your cheap affairs, mind, of amateur monkeys and two dogs and a goat, but a real, complete, elaborate, efficient circus, with just now its best artistes out to give to the town bold advertisement of its coming performance that afternoon. Four huge lumbering elephants strode along deliberately, men on their backs directing them with the touch of a stick; when an elephant lifted its trunk as though about to play something, the girls in the crowd that lined the village street shouted, "Oh—ah!" affrightedly, and stepped back on the toes of people behind them. Came, too, dainty white miniature horses, decorated with trappings and bells, and led by pages in such admirable costumes that it seemed almost a pity the wearers had not bethought themselves of shaving; handsome, proud, capering black horses ridden by sedate matrons in riding habits, who, being applauded by the lookers on, bowed graciously and touched their hats with their whips, but who, on the suggestion being loudly offered by Bobbie (now scarlet with excitement) that they should turn a somersault, frowned and looked at the crowd with the air of offended empresses. Piebald ponies, brown ponies, chestnut ponies and grey ponies, and, when you were tired of ponies, a gorgeous car with uniformed footmen walking soberly at its side, and high up in this car a lady with a trident and golden helmet and white robes, who gazed straight before her and sniffed a little, and once unfortunately gave a sneeze that sent the golden helmet a little awry, but who, despite these drawbacks (which, of course, were no reflection on her moral worth), looked a very fine and dignified figure of a woman.

"Who's she supposed to be?" asked Bobbie.

"Britannier," said the Slogger.

"I know what you mean," said Bobbie.

The small girl who had attempted to cry, and now beamed, asked if the lady was related to the Britannia, Camden Town, and found herself for her ignorance derided by the rest of the party.

"Course not, you silly young silly," replied Bobbie. "Britannia represents the country, and she's the kind of mother of us all. Ain't she, Slogger?"

"But s'pose you ain't got a muvver?" said the small girl, thinking she had detected a flaw in the argument.

"Why, that's jest where she comes in useful," declared Bobbie. "Ain't it, Slogger?"

"In a manner of speaking," acknowledged the Slogger, cautiously, "yes."

The two camels went by awkwardly, and Bobbie told the other children an amazing anecdote concerning them, invented on the spur of the moment; the performing dogs passed with ridiculous frills round their necks and an appealing look in their eyes that begged people not to laugh at them; more horses, with more haughty ladies; at the end of all the crowd fell in and followed the procession to the large canvas tent away on a triangle of spare land. As the party from Hoxton continued their march along the road to their destination, they seemed altogether different from those children who had come down. Bobbie sang. When they were clear of the town, two long pieces of string were seen far away in the broad dusty road. Coming near, the first piece of string proved to be a long procession of scarlet Tam o' Shanter capped girls; the second was found to be made up of bright round-faced expectant boys in serviceable suits, chosen in order to evade any appearance of a uniform.

"Stop," said the Slogger once more, "and watch."

"Where are they going?" asked Bobbie.

"Why, to the cirkiss," answered the Slogger. "These are only the best of 'em, though. The others 'ave to stay behind."

"They'd no business," said the boy darkly, "to make no distinction."

"Take off your cap to the ladies in charge."

"Not me," said Bobbie.

"Take it off, when I keep telling you," ordered the Slogger anxiously. "You'll only get me and yourself into a row."

"Only this once, then," said the boy.

The Tam o' Shanter capped little women, as they marched by the new arrivals, seemed much amused at the odd appearance of certain of the new recruits.

"For two pins," said Bobbie threateningly, as he noted this attitude, "I'd punch all their bloomin' 'eads."

When the string of boys came the interest appeared more pronounced, and Bobbie, too, looked anxiously to see the kind of men with whom he would in future live. He felt bound to confess that they were rather a smart set of youngsters marching along with a swing; good temper (for which the afternoon's treat was partly responsible) written large on everyone's face. One boy of the marching detachment, being distant from the two or three teachers who were in charge, asked the Slogger satirically whether he would take a bit of slate pencil for the whole fourteen, and the Slogger having no reply, Bobbie threw a stone that hit the satirical boy on the leg, causing him to cry "Wah!" The boys having passed, the small detachment from Hoxton marched on again, and presently they saw away at the side of the road a long row of red-tiled houses going into fields and nursery gardens, and giving to the flat country a look of bright importance. The Slogger spoke.

"There you are," said the Slogger, pointing. "There's 'ome sweet 'ome for all you kiddies."

The Slogger pulled a bell at the closed gateway, and on the gate opening obediently, the Slogger, with his silent colleague, entered the covered passage at the head of the fourteen youngsters. Near the end of the covered passage, a genial uniformed man met them, and saying, "Hullo! hullo! hullo!" took from the Slogger a blue form, which appeared to be a kind of bill of lading, and checked the goods carefully; then a stout motherly woman bustled out of the house, which was the first, it seemed, of the many red-tiled houses that strolled away into the meadows, and asked, "Have you wiped your boots, me dears?" and when they answered in a shy chorus, "Yus!" bade them wipe them again, a precaution justified in view of the spotless floors and well-swept passages which they presently found inside. The Slogger and his colleague had a glass of beer and some bread and cheese, and then the Slogger said "Good-bye and good luck!" his silent companion whispered with a mysterious air to Bobbie, "Long live Enarchy!" and they went.

"And now," said the uniformed gate-keeper, taking off his jacket, "now to bath one or two of you biggest boys. S'phia, pick out yours."

The wife of the uniformed man selected the girls and three of the tiniest boys, and led them away to a separate bath-room.

"'Alf a sec.," said Bobbie, protestingly. "I've had a good wash once this week."

"Once isn't often," remarked the uniformed man, opening the door of the bath-room. "You'll find that you'll not only have to wash regular, but you'll get a proper bath twice a week, besides learning to swim."

"It's carrying a 'obby to an excess," growled Bobby.

"Go in!" ordered the man. "We'll see to you first."

"That be 'anged for a tale," remarked the boy, doggedly.

For answer, Bobby found himself shot swiftly into the bath-room.

"You begin to argue," said the man, not unkindly, "and you'll get into trouble: you do what you're told, and you'll find yourself as right as rain."

This was the lesson that Bobbie at first obstinately declined to learn. The cottage was the probationary cottage where all new comers stayed in quarantine for fourteen days, with every day a visit from the doctor; the restraint and the regularity and the cleanliness and the general order of the place were foes against which Bobbie warred fiercely. He would have been more antagonistic at this stage, only that the doorkeeper's wife was a good, burly soul, with a heart as large as her hand (both were easily moved), and when one day of the fortnight she saw Bobbie comforting the small crying girl who had arrived with the detachment, by standing on his head and clapping his heels to a martial rhythm, in order that the child might be induced to change tears for laughter, and when on charging Bobbie with being a good boy to thus divert the weeping young lady, he furiously denied the imputation, then the good woman determined that there was good in Bobbie, and rewarded him with a special meat pasty that the boy could not, in justice to his appetite, refuse. Furtively, too, he made admirable dolls from young turnips which had been brought in with others from the large gardens at the back, and had been cast aside; one of these—a staring damsel, with two peas for eyes, and a broad bean for a nose—so much endeared itself to the heart of the lachrymose little girl that, one evening, in an excess of emotion, she ate it, afterwards crying her little heart out with remorse.

"And now, young Lancaster," said the doorkeeper, looking in the bathroom at the end of a fortnight that seemed about two years, "now you'll on with your clothes and come along o' me to Collingwood Cottage."

"Very near time, too," said Bobbie, rubbing himself with the towel. "I've had enough of this blooming bath nonsense."

"Oh, no, you haven't, my lad."

"I feel," grumbled the boy, "as though I never want to wash again. Where's my weskit, boss?"

"Where's your manners?" demanded the doorkeeper sharply.

"I don't trouble about manners," said Bobbie; "people 'ave to take me as they find me. If they don't like it, they can jolly well lump it."

"They'll lump you if you are not careful," warned the doorkeeper. "Rub your head again with the towel, and look sharp about it."

"They'll look silly if they come interferin' 'long o' me," said Bobbie, with the towel over his head. "I ain't like a kid."

"Yes, you are," said the man sagely. "Not only have you got a great deal to learn, but, moreover, you've got a great deal to forget. And touching this bath business, that you seem to kick against so, p'raps you'll be interested to hear that in Collingwood you'll have to wash just as regular as you've washed here, and you'll get your two baths a week without fail."

"Go on!" said the boy, uneasily.

"I'm telling you the truth, my lad. Your foster-parents 'll see to that. Your new father works in the carpenter's shop, and he's what you may call a hard man."

"If he comes the hard business with me," muttered the boy, truculently, "I'll dam well show him."

He was presently, after a kiss from the wife, which he received shamefacedly, conducted out into the broad, gravelled roadway dividing the two rows of red-roofed cottages; stop made at a clematis-covered house which bore its title over the doorway. There his new foster-mother appeared and eyed him critically, looked with great care at his head and eyes, and the hour being in school-time and the cottage therefore without family, she took him over the rooms, showing him with pride the prints from Christmas numbers on the walls, the white-floored, white-tabled dining-room, the comfortable sitting-room with its illustrated weekly papers, and the kitchen and scullery, where everything shone so that mirrors would have been a superfluity; afterwards up the broad staircase to the dormitories, each with seven red-counterpaned beds, and a floor that gave promise of some day disappearing entirely under the attacks of scrubbing from two long boys on their knees.

"And some day," said the foster-mother, generously, "if you grow up a good boy and become a half-timer, you shall be one of the two lads to stay at home and help me with the 'ouse work."

"No great catch," remarked Bobbie, grimly.

"Ah!" said the foster-mother, "you think so now; but you wait."

"It's gels' work, not men's."

"We don't 'ave girls in Collingwood," said his foster-mother.

"Good job too."

"And so I expect my boys to give me all the help about the house that they can, you see. They'll be back from school and the workshops presently, and then you'll meet 'em all."

"That'll be a treat," said the boy, satirically. "What's your name?"

"You'll call me 'mother,' and you'll call my 'usband 'father.'"

"Got some brawsted silly notions down 'ere," he said.

"Use a word like that again, my boy," said his foster-mother, with severity, "and you'll 'ave rice instead of meat for dinner."

"Like what?" asked the boy, astonished. The foster-mother spelt the word. "Not say brawsted," echoed Bobbie, amazedly. "Why, what can you say?"

Limitations of speech afflicted Bobbie sorely when the thirty boys trooped into Collingwood from school and from work, jostling him as they took their places at the dinner-table. He had become so accustomed to the use of expressive words, here tabooed, that it was not easy for him to find effective substitutes. The boys aggravated him, too, by the excellence of their spirits; to look at them and to hear them talk, one would imagine this to be the brightest and cheeriest spot on earth; Bobbie made up his mind to correct this want of balance by surly and (when opportunity should offer) aggressive behaviour. He sat at the table gloomily, and when the foster-father, who brought to the dining-room a scent of shavings, rallied him, making a mild joke upon his Christian name (affecting to mistake Bobbie for a City policeman), the boy declined to join in the laugh, and scowled persistently.

Later, at the large school-house over the way, he found himself exposed to another ordeal, one that he decided in his small brain to be nothing more nor less than a studied insult, and this was an examination in spelling, reading, and arithmetic, from which he emerged with a self-abasement equalled by indignation against the young assistant teacher who had had to put questions to him. Thanks to the care that he had always taken to evade education offered by the State, he found himself placed in a class at the end of the large school-room amongst boys who were all some years his junior; found himself, too, failing to jump difficulties which they cleared with comparative ease, and becoming in consequence the recipient of much satire. After a few weeks of consideration, he decided one morning, as he put his head under the shower-tap in the washing-room at Collingwood—he had begun to conquer his disinclination for cleanliness—that he would show everybody he was not of the stuff that butts were made; that he would apply himself seriously to the acquirement of knowledge. This fact being made apparent, the young assistant found another target for his shafts of satire, and when one afternoon the question of 7 times 7 minus 9 was put to Bobbie, and the class prepared to be exceedingly diverted at Bobbie's answer and was so diverted, not recognizing the fact that his answer proved absolutely correct, then the class had to be admonished for inappropriate hilarity, in terms that made Bobbie's little head swell with content. Being advanced to the next of the three classes in the large school-room, he had maps to wrestle with, and felt for a time a grievance against his country because it had possessions in so many quarters of the globe.

Late afternoon brought relief in the shape of drill on the large square space at the end of all the cottages and near to meadows; drill conducted by an upright ex-army man in braided uniform, who doubled the parts of a stern disciplinarian of a drill-master, and a genial distributor of goods as a storekeeper. On parade the drill-master was like a commander-in-chief (but less hampered than that official by Secretaries of State for War and people); there came exercise with Indian clubs to the music of a band of boys in uniform of blue with scarlet facings, so that at a distance you might think they belonged to the service, and who were sometimes so proud of their ability that they could scarcely play the brass instruments; real military drill with small wooden rifles, and once the awkwardness of the first few drillings passed, and once you became used to the drillmaster's voice, it was capital sport, because you had only to give imagination rein and you were a grown-up lifeguardsman with an admirable chest, chin well up, six feet two inches in your boots, and all the ladies who lived downstairs in West End houses hard at work worshipping you. Later, at five o'clock (the time being late autumn), you met the drill-sergeant again in the gymnasium, which was the swimming bath boarded over, and there you had the rarest games with parallel bars and the vaulting horse and horizontal bars, and goodness alone knew what. When all this had gone on for a few months Bobbie found to his great satisfaction that in stretching out his right arm and then bringing his fist back towards the shoulder there appeared above the elbow a distinct, palpable, unmistakable, not to be denied, sign of thick muscle. Saying his prayers that night on the reminder of the monitor of his room, he omitted the formula that he had been obliged to learn, and substituted special thanks for this development, asking that he might become a strong man, so that he could knock anybody down whenever that act should appear appropriate and desirable.

Thus Robert Lancaster grew.

## CHAPTER VI

The days in general resembled each other at the Cottage Homes, but there were exceptions. For instance, Bank Holidays. On the first Bank Holiday after the winter, came to the homes long, awkward young men who had been boys, caught years since in the streets of Shoreditch, and transferred (as Bobbie had been transferred) and educated and trained, and who being now plutocrats in the enjoyment of twenty-five shillings a week, or bandsmen capable of blowing agreeable airs in military bands, or wide-trousered sailors with a roll in their walk and brown open throats; these came to re-visit the place that had made men of them, and to salute respectfully admiring foster-parents, saying, Yes, thank you, mother, I'm getting along middling, thanks, mustn't grumble, I s'pose, and how are you, and how's father? And I've took the liberty, mother, which I trust you'll excuse, of bringing you my photograph, which I hope you'll accept with my best compliments. The foster-mother having been duly ecstatic over the photograph, ("Your nose has come out so well, boy, that's what I like about it"), there would be tea in the dining-room with some of the present boarders standing around open-eyed and open-mouthed, whilst the young man told mother amusing anecdotes of his present occupation, and fenced mother's delicate inquiries concerning the whereabouts of his heart. It was a proud young man who, the boys being ordered from the room, could bring from the breast pocket of his coat a cabinet-sized picture of an elegant young woman standing by a rustic gate with an open book in her hand (this to show that in her, literature had a friend) and an unconscious but slightly anxious look on her face as who should say, "Oh dear, dear, dear, I do hope nobody is photographing me," and to announce that this was his own, his very own young lady. The cottage having been visited, there were nurses to call upon in the detached houses in fields beyond the gate, and the masters of the school, and (with great respect) the superintendent and his wife in their house, and the doorkeeper and his wife in their cottage ("My word, I shall never forget the day I come here first"), and finally to light cigars in full view of the admiring boys and depart. Also came friends of the boys or their more or less unfortunate parents; and these, the way from Hoxton being long and places of refreshment by the way numerous, sometimes arrived at the gates in such extravagant spirits that, to the bitter sorrow of some expectant youngster within, they could not be admitted. Bobbie on a certain Easter Monday was feeling sick at the throat upon seeing other boys with friends around them, when to him were announced two ladies—Mrs. Bell and Miss Trixie Bell!

"Hello, Bobbie," cried Mrs. Bell, "don't you look a treat!"

Mrs. Bell was costumed in a manner which reflected credit not only upon herself and her dressmaker, but also in some way upon the boarder at the Cottage Homes whom she was visiting. Beneath a heavy fur-bordered cloak Bobbie could not help noting that Mrs. Bell was in blue satin; a broad band sparkling with beads went around her ample waist. Her face, it is true, had become scarlet from the exercise of walking, but this only lent a further variety of colour to her general appearance; her black bonnet escaped the charge of monotony by the presence of deftly placed yellow roses in full bloom. Her daughter, growing and already several years older in manner than her mother, was more demurely apparelled, and as she stood near her mother she drew careful diagrams on the gravel with the end of her parasol. Glancing at her, it occurred to Bobbie for the first time that Trixie Bell would become rather a fine young woman when Time had lent further aid; she was neatly gloved, her shoes were beyond criticism. One of the duties that had come with years was, it appeared, to pilot her mother, and to warn her when natural exuberance caused that good woman to approach those rocks which, in speech, cause disaster.

"I never saw such a difference in all my life," declared Mrs. Bell. "Why, you 'aven't been here a couple of years and your hands are as clean as clean."

"How are you getting on, ma'am?" he asked civilly. "Still in that little place in Pimlico Walk?"

"Me and mother," interposed Miss Bell, "think of taking a business now in the Kingsland Road."

"Ho, ho!" said Bobbie, "mixing with the upper ten, aye?"

"I 'aven't got reely used to the idea yet," confessed Mrs. Bell. "I shall miss the smell of the fried fish shop at the end dreadfully. When the wind is in the east it is quite a 'earty meal merely to look out of the doorway and sniff."

"You'd better find somewhere to sit down, mother," said her daughter, severely.

"I could do with a chair."

"Come into my cottage," said Bobbie, with pride. "This way! I'll introduce you to mother."

"I must say," remarked Mrs. Bell, as they walked along the broad space between the lines of cottages, "that I'd no idea you were so comfortable. I thought they was always thrashing of you at these schools."

"Not always," said Bobbie.

"And fed you on brimstone and treacle."

"You're thinking of the old days, mother," said Trixie. "It's all been altered since your time."

"Not, mind you," said Mrs. Bell, "that I was a charity gel. Such education as I had was got at a very high-class school off the 'Ackney Road, where you had to pay your threepence a week, and where the head-mistress—unfortunately she'd no roof to her mouth—had once upon a time been lady's maid in a very good family indeed. I don't say I'm perfect," argued the lady, "but the stigmer of being a charity—"

"Look where you're going, mother."

"Here we are," said Bobbie. "I'll just go first and see if you can come in."

Not only could they go in, but they did go in, and Mrs. Bell's astonishment at the cleanliness of the place was so frank and so genuine that the Collingwood mother instantly unbent from a rigid attitude of defence and took Mrs. Bell into the sitting-room, where over a strong cup of tea that extorted from Mrs. Bell (her be-rosed bonnet untied and the cloak loosened) further compliments, the two ladies discussed new soaps as opposed to what they called elbow grease, and found common ground in applauding the manners of thirty years ago. Bobbie and Miss Trixie Bell, thus released from attendance, strolled round the gardens, where Bobbie showed the young woman his special plot, and gave her, comme souvenir, a potato, which owed its existence and growth to his efforts. He took her to see the small room near the school, where the band practised, and confided to her his aspirations in regard to the cornet. On Trixie desiring, with some diffidence, to know what Bobbie proposed to be when he should arrive at manhood, he replied, "A sailor, very like," and Miss Bell instantly expressed her disapproval on the ground that occupation at sea took a man from his home to an extent that was scarcely convenient. Bobbie acknowledged that he had not at present made up his mind definitely, and that perhaps after all he should come back to Hoxton and dodge about and pick up a living somehow, but this plan also found disfavour in the young woman's eyes, and she argued against it with much force and eloquence until Bobbie felt bound to interfere.

"Tell you what," he said brusquely, "I shall do jest what I jolly well like."

Returning to Collingwood after this heated debate, the two appeared rather silent, and when a long red-haired girl nodded from the other side of the way to Bobbie, Miss Bell inquired curtly concerning her, to which Bobbie replied frivolously and incorrectly that her name was Montmorency, speaking of her as the lady to whom he was engaged to be married; the facts being that her name was Nutler, and that he and the ruddy-haired young lady had not yet exchanged a word with each other. Mrs. Bell found herself borne off by her perturbed daughter in the middle of an interesting description of the manner in which she lost Mr. Bell, and at the gates the good soul kissed Bobbie and gave him a shilling; the while Miss Bell walked off and assumed a languid interest in a mail cart belonging to an infant boarder. Bobbie touched his cap.

"It's my belief, Trixie," declared Mrs. Bell, before she was out of hearing, "that he'll grow up a perfect gentleman."

"Oh, will he?" said Bobbie to himself, with great artfulness. "Shows how much she knows about it."

## CHAPTER VII

Occasions when the boy allowed himself an outburst of rebellion became more rare as he felt his way slowly up the school-room to the height of the third standard; the Collingwood mother found herself able one day to congratulate him on the fact that for two months he had not imperilled his right to a meat dinner. Excellence of table proved, indeed, with all the boys in the Cottage Homes a powerful incentive to good behaviour. The bill of fare changed every day; boiled beef and carrots on (say) Thursday were followed by roast mutton on Friday and by Irish stew on Saturday, with a precise allowance to each cottage (a restriction which did not apply to vegetables), so that meals had, by reason of this variety, a charm of unexpectedness which pleased the boys greatly. In their own homes in Hoxton most of them had only been sure of two things in regard to dinner—either that there would not be enough, or that there would be none at all. Thus it was that when appeals to a boy's sense of honour or his sense of decorum failed, an appeal to his appetite proved effective. With Bobbie, moreover, there was ever, as a high goal to be strived for, the band. With the assistance of a good-natured euphonium who lived in Collingwood, and after much wrestling with obstinate difficulties, the knowledge that F.A.C.E. spelt the open spaces became his proud possession; other musical facts capitulated on seeing his determination. Whenever tempted to punch another boy's head, and roll that boy on the asphalted space where they played during the ten minutes' relief from school, and to tear that boy's pocket, and to do him grievous damage, the thought of himself marching in the band uniform and blowing the cornet part of the "Turkish Patrol" arrested his hand; the same thought did him the same good service when, on being sent to the store-keeper's room, he found himself near to an open drawer containing sugar and chocolate. At times, however, temper burst so suddenly that there was no time for the thought of cornet to intervene, and then the possibility of being allowed to join the band went away so far as to be nearly out of sight, and Bobbie mourned. On one of these grey days he happened to be despatched to the bandmaster with a note. The bandmaster was rehearsing the overture to "Zampa" in the small room overfilled with noise by twenty lads, who had become scarlet-faced from the tension of watching the slips of music before them, of watching, also, the bandmaster's beat.

"'Pon my word," cried the bandmaster explosively, rapping the stand before him with his stick, and stopping the brazen blasts that had made windows shake, "if you cornets aren't enough to make a saint forget himself. What do you think you're doing?"

Cornets, with respect, replied that they thought they were playing a tune.

"I should never have guessed that," retorted the bandmaster caustically. Bobbie delivered his note. "What you'll be like if you go out anywhere to play this summer don't bear thinking about."

One of the cornets offered the remark that he was doing his best.

"And bad's your best," cried the bandmaster explosively. "Why, I'd guarantee to take a piece of wood and make it play the cornet better than you do, Nutler." The cornet player, Nutler, here chuckled under the impression that the bandmaster required laughter in recognition of the humour of the remark. "Don't laugh at me, sir," ordered the bandmaster violently. "I won't have it." Nutler, the cornet-player, assumed a look of abject woe. "And don't look like that, either."

Master Nutler, goaded, inquired resentfully how he was to look, then.

"You're to look smart, sir," said the bandmaster, "if you want to continue in the band. There's plenty of others, mind you, ready to take your place."

Master Nutler muttered the disastrous remark that they would take a bit of finding.

"Oh!" said the bandmaster, "would they take a bit of finding?" He called to Bobbie, now leaving the room. "Boy," he cried out, "come here."

Bobbie returned and saluted.

"Have you any ear for music?"

"How d'you mean ear, sir?" asked Bobbie anxiously.

"Can you sing?"

"What'll you 'ave, sir?" said Bobbie.

"Anything."

The boy, round-eyed with eagerness, sang a few lines of an amiable glee which Collingwood boarders were accustomed to chant.

"We're gowing to the woodlands, to the woodlands gay and free. Now, who will be my comrade and come along with me? For I—"

"That'll do," said the bandmaster. "Do you think you could play a musical instrument?"

"I think I could try, sir."

"Good! You come to elementary practice this evening."

"Thank you, sir," said Bobbie, flushing delightedly.

"Now, Mr. Clever Nutler," remarked the bandmaster acutely to the cornet boy, "we'll see who's right—you or me. Come along. Let's try this second part again."

Master Nutler whispered to Bobbie as he went by that for two pins he would wring Bobbie's something neck, but the two pins not being forthcoming Master Nutler did not carry his threat into effect. Bobbie went out of the room, and as he walked by the side of the garden could not help noticing how much brighter the sun appeared, and how very excellent was the world. He grew so ecstatic over the prospect of becoming a man of importance that he wrote in the evening to the Duchess at the address given to him two years before, a letter which seemed to him to err, if anything, on the side of modesty.

"MY DEAR DUCHES,—I am writing a few lines to hope that you and Mr. Leigh are quite well and getting on fine. I have not seen you for a long pereod.

"I am pleased to tell you that I am principle player in the band here, and much esteemed by my masters and by my fellow scolars. Everybody says I shall make one of the finest music players in the world if I only go on and succede. Dear Duches, I think sometimes of the old days, but not often, because I am so busy with my music. I am an accomplished scolar and a cr. to the schools.

"If you ever come to London you can come and see me, but dress nice, and do not say nothing about Ely Place and Mr. Miller. I am in compond division. Remember me to Mr. Leigh, and I remain,—Yours truly,

"ROBERT LANCASTER.

"I shall probably play at the Flower Show in Augst. They all say the band will be nothing without me. I am now twelve years next birthday, which will be also in Augst."

Robert Lancaster took so much care in regard to behaviour after his first lesson on the cornet, and walked about with such a detached important air that the Collingwood mother insisted on giving him medicine under the impression that his health could not be perfect. An outburst of temper reassured the good lady, but general improvement was a passport that enabled Bobbie to enter the gates of her matronly reserve, and she singled him out for favour by telling him about her youth in Devonshire; memories that helped to revive Bobbie's thoughts of his one gay spell of hop-picking years ago in Kent.

The Collingwood mother, having been away from her native county for twenty years, gave idealistic descriptions of Torrington, and Milton Damerel, and Brandis Corner, so that the country generally became pictured in his mind as a land of fair delight. When Collingwood's mother shook her head in despair at being unable to describe the joys more fully, Bobbie would brag about Hoxton and the Haberdashers' School at the end of Pitfield Street, with its statue of Aske and its tall iron railings. Somehow the more he talked of the place the less inclined be felt to return there.

"Don't speak to me about your Hoxtons," begged the Collingwood mother. "Give me decent people to mix with that know how to wash 'emselves."

"They're pretty smart up there," urged Bobbie, with deference. "They know a thing or two."

"They know a thing or two too many," declared the Collingwood mother, severely. "I don't suppose you've ever come across the worst of 'em, but I'm told there are thieves and coiners, and goodness knows what all about the place."

"Think it's a fact, mother?" inquired Bobbie with innocence.

"Bless you, yes. The lowest of the low. Didn't you never come across any of them?"

"Me?" echoed the boy. "Goo' gracious! What a question to ask."

"Perhaps you were too young to take notice."

"That might have been it," he conceded. "Fact of the matter is my real mother was very careful who she mixed with, and there might 'a been railway snatchers or anything around us for all I knew."

"Don't talk about them," interrupted the Collingwood mother, shivering. "Let me tell you some more about Devonshire."

Summer came to the Cottage Homes and brought with it cricket matches to be played against the boys of the private school a few meadows off, where the two different grades of young men met on common ground that the best of games offers, and where Bobbie developed an ability for bowling slows of a peculiarly artful and delusive character, insomuch that they came from his hand in a way that made the batter (confident of hitting a six-er) run out to strike, with the result that he not infrequently found himself bowled or stumped. These games with boys of happier circumstances did much to refine the lads of the Cottage Homes; even Bobbie, whilst he ridiculed and burlesqued some of the private school youths who had a languid way of talking and a courteous behaviour, found himself selecting some of the tricks of manner that seemed to him worthy and commendable, and these improved him. The cornet helped.

Rehearsals of the band became more furious as the day of the Flower Show approached. Master Nutler by dint of successful experiments in insubordination found his engagement for the event in peril, and Master Nutler had more than once pressed Bobbie to decide the question of their musical ability by a stand-up fight. Quite a large family of Nutlers lived in the Homes, ranging from the lanky, red-haired girl of fifteen to a baby of two; the father and mother of the family having, on retirement to an unknown quarter, generously presented their entire quiver-full to the guardians as souvenir of indebtedness to their native parish, so that a sample of the Nutler family could he found in nearly every cottage and in the ophthalmic hospital beyond the gates. The gauge of combat being thrown down repeatedly in the presence of witnesses, Bobbie felt bound at last to take it up, and arrangements being effected by a mature boy, the fight took place furtively in the kitchen garden one evening at twilight; Bobbie punishing Master Nutler so effectively that he had to give that weeping indignant young gentleman two glass alleys, a china apple, and a copy of a book from the Index Expurgatorius, in order to prevent him from saying anything about it. Master Nutler, thus bribed, generously agreed not to report the circumstance to the authorities, but he gave information to the other members of his family, and commanded a vendetta against Robert Lancaster. The Nutler family had its private differences; indeed, its members seldom met without quarrelling, but in the presence of an opportunity for spite against a common enemy they united, and conferred amicably on a course of action. The eldest Miss Nutler favoured scratching of the enemy's face; after debate the others induced her to withdraw this resolution, and to agree to a plan of more elaborate strategy.

Gay expectation scented the air on the morning of the Flower Show. For the band especially, it meant occupying on a sunlit lawn a position of conspicuous importance, to be followed by admirable feeding and iced lemonade that had no limits except those fixed by the band's own capacity. It was an occasion, too, when fair ladies came from mansions of the neighbourhood and paid graceful compliments to the band, sometimes giving to members bright, alluring pieces of silver. Master Nutler, who had received intimation that, owing to his want of care at rehearsals, his services would not be required, when about muttering to himself in a gruff undertone, as men will when they are suffering from repressed grievances. At twelve o'clock, after morning school, the conscientious bandmaster took the boys through the devious ways of the "Il Trovatore" selection, and piloted them with the solo parts of "H.M.S. Pinafore." Bobbie's playing of his solo extorted from the bandmaster a rare word of approval.

"You've got on wonderfully well, Lancaster," said the bandmaster.

"Thanks to you, sir," said the boy politely.

"You aren't quite so steady as I could wish, but I think you'll pull through."

"You leave it to me," said Bobbie, rubbing the cornet affectionately with his handkerchief.

"At two o'clock, boys, we start. Take care that none of you get into a mischief between now and then." A chorus of assurances. "Ah!" sighed the bandmaster, "I know what boys are. Lancaster, can you take a note to the superintendent for me?"

"Like a shot, sir."

Bobbie, flying out into the asphalted playground to take the note in the promised manner, found himself tripped up by Master Nutler, who, having done this, demanded, with great indignation, to know where Bobbie was a-coming to. Bobbie replied that some day, when he could afford it, he proposed to enjoy the pleasure of again wiping the floor with Nutler, whereupon that young gentleman requested that the task should not be postponed, but should be effected at once. Bobbie forced himself into composure, and hurried on, followed by a parting remark from Nutler, "Sneak!"

Trotting along by the fringe of flower beds on the right-hand side of the broad walk, in great good-humour, the scream of a girl near to one of the red-roofed houses made him stop. Lanky Miss Nutler, having seen him approach, had twisted the arm of the small girl who, two years previously, had arrived at the Homes with Bobbie, and who, having long since given up tears, had become one of the brightest little maids in the place. At present, however, she appeared terrified out of her usual cheerfulness because of superfluous attention paid to her by Miss Nutler.

"Now will you be good?" inquired Miss Nutler, suavely, as she gave the small girl's arm another twist.

"I am good," cried the small girl piteously. "Leave off twistin' my wrist, or else I shall have to scream."

"Promise not to call me Miss Camel again," ordered the lanky young woman.

"I never did."

"I shall punish you," said Miss Nutler, with regret, "more for telling a lie than for calling me out of my proper name." The small girl screamed with pain. "Ah! you may 'oller."

"Leave the girl alone," shouted Bobbie from the fence of the garden.

"Beg your pardon?" said Miss Nutler, with studied courtesy. "I didn't quite catch what you said."

"Leave that little girl alone," he repeated sharply. "If she's done anything wrong, it's for others to punish her, not you."

"I don't wish to 'old any conversation with you," said the young woman sedately. "Kindly mind your own business."

"Leggo my wrist," cried the small girl agonizedly. "Come and make her, Bobbie Lancaster. She'll—she'll break my arm."

Master Lancaster darted through the gates. The small girl's face was white with pain; Miss Nutler's face yellow with defiance. He released the small girl quickly, and she ran off. Miss Nutler staggered hack, and fell, an ungraceful heap, on the ground.

"'Elp! 'Elp! Murder!" yelled Miss Nutler. "Fi—yer!"

"Now what are you kicking up a row for?" demanded Bobbie.

"He's killed me," declared Miss Nutler, panting, to the mother of her cottage, who had hastened out to ascertain the cause of disturbance. "Oh, the villain! Oh, fetch a doctor! Oh, don't let him make his escape!"

"I'm not going to make no escape," said the boy sturdily. "I never knocked her down; she fell down."

"Oh!" cried Miss Nutler. "To think that he should tell a untruth. Oh, I wonder he ain't struck down before my very eyes! Oh, I'm going into 'sterricks!"

And she went off into what, it must be admitted, was, for a young amateur, a very fair imitation of a hysterical fit.

The mother, much concerned, told Bobbie that he would have to be taken at once to the Superintendent. The father of a cottage opposite appeared. Interference by boys with girls, said the father, was just the one thing that had to be punished for more than anything. Could not be permitted for a single moment—not for a single moment.

"Why, what's anyone to do," stammered the boy, indignantly, "when they see a big girl like her ill-using another 'alf her size?"

The father said that it was not for Bobbie to interfere.

"I simply separated of 'em," pleaded the boy. "She was using the little girl something crool, and—"

"Perjerer!" interrupted Miss Nutler, reviving for this purpose. She closed her eyes again, and hammered at the ground with her heels.

"And I particular don't want to get into no trouble just now. I'll explain it all to-morrow."

The father said that to-morrow would not do. Bobbie must go along with him now to the Superintendent's house, the while the mother would use her best endeavours to restore Miss Nutler. The latter task proved to be one of no difficulty, for the young woman, on the palms of her hands being slapped, re-opened her eyes, and said, faintly,—

"Where am I? Tell me, someone! Is it all a 'orrible dream?"

The Superintendent, ordinarily a cheery man, whistled gravely as he listened to the report against the boy standing at the other end of the table.

"Thought you were a good lad, Lancaster."

"Not much use being good, sir," growled Bobbie, "when your luck's against you."

The father, an old policeman, enjoying this echo of the old days, repeated and added to his report of Miss Nutler's condition, remarking sagely that extreme violence must have been used.

"We'll investigate it fully to-morrow," commanded the Superintendent. "No time now. Meanwhile you'll stay at home, my lad."

"What?" said Bobbie, amazedly. "And not play at the show?"

"And not play at the show. Some one else must be found to take your place. I'm sorry."

The boy swallowed something in his throat, and his under lip twitched. He looked round at the framed list of rules on the wall, at the papers on the table, and at everything in the room with a dazed air.

"I'm a—a bit sorry about it, too," he said gloomily.

"Rules are rules," mentioned the Superintendent.

"Someone shall suffer for it," declared the boy, with sudden fierceness. "I ain't going to be jumped on just because—"

"Take him down to Collingwood," ordered the Superintendent.

"Can't you give me a good wolloping, sir, and have done with it?"

"Take him away, please."

It was a fierce and an aggrieved and a revengeful lad who looked out of the window of Collingwood that afternoon and watched the band marching out towards the gates, uniformed in its best, and carrying its instruments proudly. The rays of the bright sun reflected in the shining brass, and Robert Lancaster blinked as he looked at them, but he did not cry, because, when he saw Nutler marching with cornet in hand, his hot little brain racked with a burning sense of injustice. He went upstairs and watched the short line of boys until trees intervened. He had some vague idea of breaking everything in the cottage that could be broken, but a moment's consideration informed him that this as a remedy would be imperfect. The mother called to him, offering some work in cleaning the grate, and Bobbie, setting to this with great strenuousness, produced such excellent results that the mother gave him her sympathy for his present situation, and joined him in denouncing Miss Nutler in good set terms. Nevertheless, the grievance remained, and the mother went so far in her cordial agreement that, after a while, the grievance appeared to have grown enormously, and he felt himself to be the very worst used man in the whole world. Somebody's head should be punched for this; if he had Teddy Sullivan's revolver, a more convincing action could be adopted. It would be rather fine and dramatic to go out when the band returned and, covering them with a six-shooter, force them to hold up their hands and give him full apology for the wrong that had been done to him. Failing the presence of an arm of warfare, it seemed not easy to see what he could do. All that he could decide in his aggrieved, blazing, infuriated mind was that he would do something.

When a post letter came at about four o'clock addressed to him in a strange old-fashioned writing, he did not at first open it, because, rare as letters were, he felt gloomily that nothing like good fortune could come to him on that day. He tore the envelope after a while, and prepared himself for another shaft of ill-luck. A postal order dropped out, and his anticipations whirled round.

"MY DEAR BOBBIE,—I were glad to hear from you, and to know that you was getting on so well in the world. My husband were also greatly pleased. He is now what is called a landoner, and is much occupied during the day looking after the men that is employed under him.

"Dear Bobbie, you must know that we live in an immense hotel, and that I ride to the hounds every day of my life. We also intertain the gentry of the neighbourhood, who treat us as their equals or more. We are not proud of our good fortune, for we know that pride cometh before a fall. I enclose a trifle to buy yourself something; I could easily send more, as we are, so to speak, roling in money, but I am in a hurry to catch the post.

"My husband sends his best respects, and hopes you will continue to grow up a good boy and respect your elders.—Yours affect'ly,

"L. LEIGH.

"Fond love and kisses."

Bobbie read this friendly and agreeable letter from the Duchess three times. Then, looking at the address carefully, he started up with a sudden inspiration.

"I know what I'll do," he said to himself excitedly. "I'll bunk off."

He made his preparations with haste, having a vague fear that something might happen to induce him to change his mind. The mother of Collingwood Cottage was dozing in her kitchen as he came downstairs, and he had a good mind to kiss the good soul; but he knew that doing this might twist his determination, and he set his mouth hard. He stuffed his small bundle under his waistcoat, and went across to the band-room with the stolid face of a man obeying orders.

"Please, I've got to take my cornet and get down to the Flower Show as sharp as I possibly can."

The same story contented the gate-keeper, who gave him the correct time, and Bobbie started along the white road at a quick pace. At the first turning he branched off, and, skirting the fields belonging to the Cottage Homes, returned to the town, where a post-office was to be found. There he changed the postal order. In five minutes he was speeding away Londonwards, with defiant head well out of the carriage windows, a cigarette between his lips, the cornet and his handkerchiefed bundle in his hand.

"This," said the boy truculently to the distant red-roofed homes, "this'll let you see what a man can do when he's put upon."


CHAPTER VIII

The confusing eddy of people outside Liverpool Street Station startled him, so that he stood back to let them go by, until he remembered that they did not cease to flow before midnight, and then he laughed at himself and made his way out into Bishopsgate. He had a fine sense of freedom in the consciousness that he was his own master; within wide limitations he could go where he pleased and do as he pleased, and no one had the right to say him nay. It seemed like getting rid of a suit of armour. He gave himself the luxury of swearing softly as he walked along, in order to prove conclusively that he was no longer trammelled by the code of rules that obtained at the Cottage Homes. Walking up towards Shoreditch Church it appeared to the boy that he was as fine a fellow as any in the crowd of men hurrying along the pavement, that his daring and his independence were sufficient for about six ordinary men; he felt very much inclined to stop one or two in order to tell them so. The better to live up to his new character of a regular blade, he turned into the saloon bar of a gorgeous, over-mirrored, over-painted, over-furnished public-house, and addressing a superb young lady who behind the bar read a pamphlet called "An Amusing Way to Pick up Biology," asked in a deep, effective voice for a sherry and bitters. The superb young lady, seemingly dazed with study, gave him instead a small bottle of lemonade and a hard biscuit; Bobbie, awed by her appearance, did not dare to complain of the mistake. He endeavoured, however, to entice the large young woman into manly conversation by asking her how long it was since she had left the old place, but she only answered absently, without looking up from her hook, "Outside with those bootlaces, please," and Bobbie refrained from repeating his question.

At the corner of Drysdale Street he met a first friend in the person of Niedermann, otherwise Nose, grown ridiculously tall, and garbed in a frock coat queerly short at the sleeves. Niedermann did not know him at first, but when recognition came he became at once interested, and asked a number of questions, some of which Bobbie answered truthfully.

"What you ought to go and do, ole man," said Niedermann, acutely, "is to disguise yourself."

"How d'you mean disguise myself?"

"Why, put on a false beard," said the frock-coated lad, "and blue spectacles, and what not. You'll get copped else."

"They won't trouble," said the boy uneasily.

"Take my advice or not, jest as you like. But I know what I should do."

"Very likely they're glad to get rid of me," argued Bobbie. "It'll be a saving to them of pounds a year, and besides—"

"Tell you what you could do," said Master Niedermann, looking at him thoughtfully, "and that too without no trouble. You see this coat and weskit of mine."

"I see what there's left of 'em."

"Swop!" said the long youth walking with Bobbie down towards the railway arch. "These what I've got are a bit short for me, because I'm a grown lad, as you may see. But they'll suit you a treat, and, besides, if they circulate your description, no one in these togs 'll recognize you for a moment."

"Wouldn't see me if I was to get inside of 'em."

"I think you're wrong," said Niedermann patiently. "What did you say the address was that you've run away from?" Bobbie gave the information. "I shall remember."

"You've no call to remember," said the boy sharply.

"I carry it all 'ere," said Master Niedermann darkly, tapping his unwashed forehead; "regular store'ouse of information my brain is."

"What makes you call it a brain?" asked Bobbie.

"Do you particularly want your 'ead punched?" asked Master Niedermann fiercely. "Because, if so, you've only got to say the word, and—" He recovered himself with an effort. "But putting all argument a one side," he said genially, "you try on my coat and see how it fits."

On Bobbie complying, Master Niedermann took no pains to conceal his approval of the change.

"My word!" he said, "you might a been measured for it by a West-End tailor."

"Ain't it a bit long in the tails?" asked Bobbie.

"All the better for that," declared the long youth with enthusiasm. "They're wearing 'em long."

"Now give me back my jacket," said Bobbie.

"That be 'anged for a tale," answered Niedermann, with an injured expression. "A bargain's a bargain."

"But this isn't a bargain," expostulated the boy in the frock-coat. "I never said—"

"Look here," said the long youth threateningly. "Do you want me to give you up to the police?"

After the interview with Master Niedermann Bobbie determined to avoid friends for the rest of that evening. He therefore walked about the streets of Hoxton, his cornet wrapped in a newspaper under his arm, dodging when he saw a face known to him. He glanced at himself on passing shop windows, and tried to believe that the frayed frock-coat gave him an increased air of manliness. Strolling cautiously into Pimlico Walk, and inspecting the little bonnet shop kept by Eliza Bell, he saw Trixie at the counter; her black hair rolled up and arranged carefully above her pretty neck, she wore a pink blouse with neat collar and cuffs, her face had a touch of colour, and Bobbie for the first time felt that he would like to kiss her. He knew, however, that to enter the shop of Mrs. Bell would necessitate listening to reproof and good advice, neither of which things was that evening desired by him. The same motive stopped him from taking a 'bus to Fetter Lane to call upon Myddleton West, whose address he remembered; he told himself that he enjoyed liberty too much to allow it to be checked by sage counsels. Going up to Ely Place and turning, with some idea of going through in order to see the house where he had spent some of his life, he had but passed the dwarf posts at the entrance when at least six separate and offensive odours rushed furiously at him. He coughed and turned back.

But in the Theatre of Varieties he found joy. He paid a shilling to the old lady in the pay box up the sawdust-covered steps, and on the old lady shouting, "Jimes," James in uniform just inside the swing doors of the crowded, heated music hall, said, "Yessir. This way, sir. Stand a one side, please, and let the genelman pass," and conducted Bobbie ceremoniously past the folk who were standing at the back of the first balcony; unlocked the door, showed him into the box; fetched a programme, accepted twopence with a military salute, called Bobbie "Me lord," evidently mistaking him for a member of the aristocracy. Then the boy settled down on the front bench in the box, preparing to enjoy himself. Fine to see the upturned faces from the twopenny pit—they sat down in the pit now, he observed; in his day you had to stand—the rows and rows of interested faces in the twopenny gallery, and to note that many of them were watching him, the only occupant of the shilling boxes. He felt confused at first with this attention. Shielding himself behind the dusty curtains, he gazed at Mlle. Printemps, who, with paper rose in her hair, bare arms, bare shoulders, and scarlet tights, kept her footing on a large white marble globe, juggling the while with plates and knives and bottles. Once or twice Mlle. Printemps, who was a little thin, perhaps, and red at the elbows, but an agreeable person for all that, came over on the great white globe quite close to the box in which Bobbie was seated, whereupon he said softly (being a desperate sort of rattle out for the evening), "I'll 'ave your flower, miss," and felt relieved to find that the thin lady on the globe had not overheard him. Then came Bray and Wilkins, described on the yellow slip as Irish-American duettists, the finest humorists of two hemispheres, whose humour was not, perhaps, so much fine as broad, being conducted somewhat in this way: Bray, facing the audience, shouted, "Oi say; have you heard about me wife?" and Wilkins, also facing the audience, shouted back, "Oi have not heard about your wife;" after a whispered communication, Wilkins assumed incredulity, and said, "Oi don't believe it, sorr," and Bray, indignant, said, "It's the truth I'm giving ye; a fine bouncing boy at eighteen minutes past five." "Oi'll not believe it," persisted Wilkins, "it's all your kid," to which Bray replied indignantly, "It's not my kid, sorr," and Wilkins retorted at once, "Who's kid is it, then?" Followed, tremendous personal chastisement, which made Bobbie laugh until tears came. After the American duettists, Mr. Tom Somebody came shyly on the stage, affecting to be astonished at finding himself there and rather wishful to go off again, but, on being humorously appealed to by the conductor, deciding to stay. Mr. Tom Somebody had been jilted by the lady of his heart, and it seemed to the judicial observer that the lady might have found excuse for her conduct in the singular manner of apparel the gentleman wore, for he had no hat, but only the brim of a hat, his jacket was very short, and his trousers very baggy; a paper front stuck out ludicrously at his chest, and—this made Bobbie shriek with delight—he had in the hurry of dressing placed his collar around his waist.

"For she's a daisy,
She sends me crazy,
No wonder people say I'm getting pline;
She only flouts me,
And sometimes outs me,
I'm goin' simply barmy on account of Emmer-jine."

At half-past eight the band played the National Anthem; the attendants shouted the order for dispersal, and Bobbie, giving up the private box with a sigh, followed the crowd down the stone staircase. Outside, the patrons of the second performance waited impatiently in a line at the edge of the pavement. Bobbie recognized one or two faces in the crowd; they looked older, he thought, and slightly dirtier; those whom he remembered as boys of about his own age were accompanied by young ladies, whose bare heads shone with oil, and who wore, for the most part, maroon-coloured dresses, partly shielded by aprons; they seemed in excellent spirits, and shouted defiant badinage to friends at a distance. To Bobbie walking down towards Old Street, it occurred that the true touch of manliness would not he achieved until he secured the company of a member of the opposite sex. He went into a tobacconist's shop and bought a twopenny cigar, with a paper belt, which he selected from a box labelled "The Rothschild Brand," and smoking this, he, with the cornet placed in the capacious tail pocket of the frock-coat, strolled through Shoreditch to Hackney Road. He winked at one or two young women hurrying home with hot suppers laid on pieces of paper, but they only sneered at him, one lady of about thirteen declaring indignantly that, were her hands not full, she would fetch him a clip side the ear.

"It's this blooming coat," said Bobbie ruefully.

These repulses brought disappointment, but happily there existed other ways of proving to the world that he was now thoroughly grown up. He went into a quiet public-house, where, in the private bar, some bemused men were talking politics, and on the invitation of the anxious young proprietor, who appeared to be new to the business and desirous of obtaining custom, Bobbie gave his opinion on the question of increasing the strength of the Navy, and, encouraged by beer, found himself quite eloquent. So eloquent, indeed, that presently he insisted upon contradicting everybody, and some unpleasantness ensued.

"You'll 'scuse me, my boy," said a white-faced, sleepy-eyed baker, pointing unsteadily at Bobbie with the stem of his pipe, "you'll 'scuse me if I take the lib'ty of tellin' you—or rather I sh' say, informing you—that you're a liar."

"You repeat that," said Bobbie, flushed and aggressive. "Go on! Say that again and see what 'appens."

"It was only meant as a pleasant joke, I expect," urged the young proprietor nervously from the other side of the counter. "Shake 'ands and make it up."

"Let him call me that again," said the boy fiercely. "That's all. I'll learn him, the—"

"What'd I call you?" inquired the tipsy baker. "Best of my rec'lection I called you hon'ble young genleman. Do you deny, sir, that you're hon'ble young genleman? Because, if so," added the baker with great solemnity, "if so, I shall have great pleasure in—hic—drinkin' your 'ealth."

"I've been insulted!" shouted the scarlet-faced boy violently, "in the presence of gentlemen! I want this put right! I want an apology! I'm as good a man—"

"Look 'ere," interrupted the anxious young publican. "'Ave a ceegar at my expense, and let bygones be bygones."

"My young friend," said the baker, balancing to and fro as he rested one hand on the zinc counter, "if I've 'pologized to you in any way, I can only say that it's purely cler'cal error on my part, and I'm prepared to most humbly insult—"

"You mean," corrected the young publican, "that if you've insulted him you're prepared to apologize."

"Dammit," cried the baker, turning explosively on the young proprietor, "can't two genlemen settle their pers'nal disputes without a blooming pot'ouse keeper dictatin' to 'em? What?"

"Yes," said Bobbie, not to be outdone, "what th' 'ell do you—"

"You mistook my meanin', gentlemen," said the young publican penitently. "All I want is peace and quietness."

"Precious rum way you've got of going about it," said Bobbie truculently. "You take my advice, Mr. Public-house, and don't you interfere with whatever matters there may be in this world that don't in no wise whatsoever tend to concern you."

"Spoke," declared the tipsy baker, offering his hand to Bobbie; "spoke like a norator. Give us a song, ole man."

"Gentlemen, I do hope—"

"Can't give you a song," said the flushed boy; "but I can give you a tune on the cornet."

"Please, gentlemen, do not—"

"Music of the cornet," declared the bemused baker, "is like gen'le dew of 'eaven. You blow up, my boy."

To the terror of the young publican, Bobbie produced his cornet and played a verse of "Tom Bowling," causing the baker to become maudlin, and to declare tearfully that he wished he had been a sailor instead of an adjective baker, trampled on by most and scorned by all. On Bobbie playing the prelude to the first set of some quadrilles, the private bar, standing up tipsily, set to partners and went through the evolutions with intense gravity, excepting the baker, who, acting as M.C., stumbled in and out crying loudly, "La'ies' chain!" The agitated young publican, fearful of consequences, felt constrained at last to send for a policeman, and when one came and touched the boy cornet player on the shoulder, saying, "Outside with that instrument of torture, if you please," then Bobbie stepped out of the swing doors and through a small crowd with the proud consciousness that, having been ejected from a public-house, real manhood was now his, and could never be taken from him. He stumbled along Hackney Road with his cornet, a slip of a crowd following. To escape them he jumped clumsily on a tram.

"'O' tight," said the conductor.

The boy rode in a confused state of mind to the end of the journey at Lea Bridge Road, and then, partly sobered by the night air, returned by the tram. He felt quite happy; other passengers found themselves afire with curiosity to know what he was laughing about. Watching the lighted shops and the cheerful folk on the pavement below, Bobbie decided hilariously that this was better than the Cottage Homes. This was good. This was enjoyment. This was independence. This was freedom. This was life.

At Cambridge Heath Station he descended, because be saw outside a large public-house a line of brakes decorated with branches of trees and with Chinese lanterns; joyous men and women danced on the square space to no music. This seemed the kind of movement in which he desired to be. The men and women had been out into the country for the day; they appeared to have brought a good deal of the country back with them, for their hats and bonnets and clothes were decorated with bunches of flowers and oak leaves. The appearance of the boy with his cornet was welcomed with enthusiasm. Hoisted up on a huge empty cask, he, by command, played gustily a waltz that made the couples lay heads on their partners' shoulders and move slowly, dreamily around. Of all the moments of pure delight that Bobbie, as a boy, was to experience, this ever stood in his memory high and high above all the rest. Presently the whirling crowd stopped exhaustedly.

"Ask the little boy," suggested one of the panting women, "to play a what's-a-name tune."

"A comic?"

"No, no, no! Not a comic. You know what I mean, only you're so stupid."

"A love tune?"

"Bah!" said the lady, "you're like all the men; you've got no sense. What I mean is a patriotic song."

Therefore, "Rule Britannia" from the cornet to the great content of the beanfeasters and of the two or three constables, looking on at the scene good-naturedly. A hat went round before the party re-ascended the brakes, and Bobbie found himself in possession of a load of coppers that weighed him down on one side until he bethought himself of the ingenious plan of dividing them and placing one half in each pocket of his trousers. He saw the brakes depart, and was about to leave when he found his arm seized violently.

"I've got him," shrieked Master Niedermann fiercely. "I thought I should find him. Evil doers never succeed for long. I was sure—"

"Leggo my arm," said Bobbie.

"Likely thing," screamed the long youth satirically, "after I've took all this trouble to find you. Gimme back my frock coat! Gimme back my frock-coat, that you pinched from me! Gimme back—"

One of the constables stepped forward. What was all this about?

"Sergeant," cried Master Niedermann flatteringly, "thank goodness you're 'ere. You'll see that right's done. He's robbed me of my best frock-coat, and I want it back."

"It's a lie," declared Bobbie. "Fact of the matter is—"

"Accuses me now," said the estimable youth, with a pained air, "of telling a falsehood. Why, I couldn't tell a falsehood, and well you know it, inspector."

Constable begged to say that he knew nothing of the kind. Let the boy tell his tale.

"We changed coats, sir," said Bobbie, "against my wish, and—"

"There's alf a dollar sewed in the corner of it," interrupted Nose, "and he must 'ave known it, or else he'd never 'ave thrown me down on the ground and clutched my neck with both his hands—like so— and then pulled the coat bodily off of me."

Constable, his legal mind detecting an error in the statement, asked, in view of the fact that the boy had but two hands, how this was done.

"Ast him!" said Master Niedermann. "He knows! He did it. And make him gimme back my coat and my 'alf dollar."

Constable requested to be informed how the half dollar had been earned or obtained.

"Be the sweat of me brow," declared the long youth. "How d'ye think? I'd forgot where I put it for the moment, or else he should never have had it. And if he don't give it me, I give him in charge."

"'Ang me if I give it back," said Bobbie, with sudden asperity. "You said a bargain's a bargain, and so it'll 'ave to be. I shan't change again."

"Then," said Master Niedermann, oracularly, "I 'ereby beg to give him into custody."

The constable seemed undecided. Bobbie watched his face, and trembled as he observed a slight increase in gravity. The police station meant at least an ignominious return to the Homes, and to the precise and dogmatically ordered life there. A crowd had gathered round close to the disputant parties, and Bobbie, withdrawing his anxious glance from the policeman for a moment to look around, saw a very little woman, whose face he remembered. Miss Threepenny. Her queer head came to about the waists of the people standing near to her.

"I suppose I'd better," said the constable.

"Twenty-five, Barton Buildings," whispered little Miss Threepenny. Then, with a quick change of voice and manner, "Who's got my purse? Who's stole my purse? Police! Stop thief! 'Elp—'elp—'elp!"

The constable hurried quickly from the doubtful case on which he was engaged to this that appeared more definite. In the commotion, Bobbie, holding his cornet tightly, made swift escape; he had reached Bethnal Green Road before Miss Threepenny—having discovered that her purse had, after all, not been stolen—had apologized to the constable for the unnecessary trouble that she had given. Bobbie was still recovering breath at the entrance to the giant block of model dwellings to which Miss Threepenny had hurriedly directed him, when that excellent little woman trotted up.

"You're a nice young man," said Miss Threepenny severely, "I don't think. Going and getting yourself mixed up in a common street row, and forgetting what you owe to your poor dead mother and—"

Bobbie explained truthfully, and little Miss Threepenny relented.

"What are you going to do now?" she asked, looking up at him with less acerbity.

"Get a bed in a coffee shop, I s'pose," said the boy. "To-morrow I shall get off to the country to see—to see some friends. This bloomin' London makes my nut ache."

The small woman stood on the third step of the stone stairs, so that she came thus face to face with Bobbie. She swung her key round her finger, reflectively.

"You'll only get into more trouble," she said.

"Likely as not," replied the boy recklessly. "I can't do right, somehow."

"I've nearly 'alf a mind," said the little woman, "to make you up a bed in my sitting-room."

"Got two rooms now, Miss?"

"Rather," said the little woman proudly.

He followed Miss Threepenny upstairs, through passages, and up more stairs to her rooms. There the diminutive woman took off her bonnet and set to work, as she said, to put the place to rights, which, seeing that everything was perfectly neat and in order, seemed a superfluous act, and indeed consisted mainly in moving the furniture from it's proper place and setting it back again. Bobbie felt confused and very tired, but the little woman appeared so obviously glad to have someone to talk to that he listened politely to her good-tempered chatters. They had supper together, and then Miss Threepenny did something to an elderly easy chair in the manner of an expert conjuror, whereupon it instantly changed into a middle-aged couch. She bustled in and out of her own room, bringing a pillow and some sheets; presently Bobbie found that he could no longer look at the couch without yawning desperately.

"In the morning," said the tiny woman, lighting a candle, "you sleep on, because I shall be out and about early. And I shall be 'ome midday to give you your dinner."

"Goo' night," said the boy sleepily, taking his coat off.

"Dear, dear!" cried the little woman with a comic affectation of bashfulness. "Do wait till I'm out of the room. You forget that I'm an old maid. Some of you young men nowadays are enough to shock a saint."

"Don't you wish you'd got a son of your own, miss?" asked Bobbie, "to live here and look after you?"

"Stuff and nonsense!" she answered quickly. "What should I want with a great big slab of a boy knocking about the place? There's a ridiculous idea to be sure! Wonder what put that into your head, for goodness' sake."

"Nothing special," said the boy, yawning. "Goo' ni'."

"All the same," said the little woman hesitatingly, "if you like, Bobbie, you can do this. Jest for fun, you know. You can give me a kiss on the forehead and say, 'Good night, mother.'" She laughed awkwardly. "Only for the lark of the thing, you know."

"Good night, mother," said the boy obediently, bending down and kissing her above the eyes. The little woman gasped and ran quickly to her room.

In the morning Bobbie awoke, when at six o'clock Miss Threepenny was at work still setting the place to rights, and arranging, as he quietly noticed, his breakfast. As she came over to him, before going off, and looked down at him, he kept his eyes half-closed. When presently he had risen, and had eaten his breakfast, he made out an account on the back of an envelope thus, and laid the money upon it:—

| | |
|---|---|
| Bread | 1d. |
| 2 saussages | 2d. |
| Tea | 1d. |
| Lodgings | 3d. |
| Tot. | 7d. |

With thanks.

R. L.

He took his cornet and went out, down the stone stairs very quietly.


CHAPTER IX

The boy discovered in London that day how much possession of a little money helps enjoyment. One does not want very much in London, but one does want some, and Bobbie, with four or five shillings in his pocket, found delights that London millionaires can never encounter. Two shillings and threepence of his fortune went to the purchase in City Road of a hard felt hat. The proprietor of the shop urged him to purchase a silk hat, and the boy tried one on, laughing very much at his own reflection in the mirror, but there were several good reasons why he should not agree with the proprietor ("A silk hat," argued the proprietor, "tells me that a man's a gentleman"), of which one was that he remembered reading a reply to a correspondent in one of the newspapers at Collingwood Cottage, which stated that a silk hat was not "de rigueur" for the country or the seaside; a second that he did not possess more than half the amount required for the cheapest specimen. The bowler hat, however, brought great content. Later in the day, finding himself in Hyde Park, he fastened his long frock-coat as well as the existing buttons would permit, and strolled down the Row, lifting his hat now and again to no one with great courtesy. He became exceedingly wishful to find some person with whom he might talk. He was getting on rather well with a little six-year-old maid, and had made for her fair-haired doll a couch of grass near the Achilles statue, and the little girl had told him that she had such a booful mamma and such a horrid large nurse and such a fearfully hard piano and such oceans of toys, when she and her doll were whisked away magically by the large nurse referred to, and Bobbie spent two whole hours in searching for them with no success. Out in Knightsbridge a string of sandwich men walked along gloomily, bearing advertisements of a new piece at one of the West End theatres; it occurred to the boy that it would be rather a fine, lordly act to pay his shilling and go to a first-class play, just for all the world as though he lived in Belgravia. The idea clipped his fancy, and despite the fact that after dinner at a cheap restaurant, whose proud boast was, "Come in here, and you will never go anywhere else," he found that he would only have just enough left to pay his fare to the nearest railway station to Brenchley, he made up his mind to go to the theatre. He had a good wash at the cheap restaurant, and parted his hair in the middle, looking very closely to see if there existed a suspicion of down upon his upper lip. It was magnificent, this life of independence, but, obviously, there were drawbacks. For instance, you had not only to arrange for your meals, but you had also to pay them; this done, the fact remained that neither the quantity nor the quality proved so good as in the Cottage Homes. The boy foresaw (without troubling himself very much about it) that herein might be found a source of inconvenience. He packed the cornet very carefully in a borrowed newspaper; the cornet was slightly in the way, but he remembered that it belonged to the Cottage Homes, and he meant to return it there eventually. It was wrong to steal.

At the gallery door of the theatre that evening he found himself in a short queue, side by side with a thoughtful-looking youth, who carried on his arm an aged travelling rug. This youth talked very learnedly to Bobbie about the new phases of the drama, Bobbie listening with respect because it was a subject on which he felt himself to be not completely informed.

"Convention," said the thoughtful young man, covering both of his arms with the old travelling rug and edging nearer to the two ladies in front, "convention, my dear sir, is the curse of the modern drama. The drama is enwrapped with iron shackles, and it screams aloud—excuse me, madam, they're pushing at the back—and it screams aloud, 'Release my bonds and give me liberty.'"

"I see," said Bobbie.

"What we want is to see the realities of life placed upon the stage," went on the thoughtful youth, "not a transparent imitation. We require the stage to give up its great services to the threshing out of some of the world's trying problems, and to—"

"Best piece I ever see was at the Britannia, 'Oxton," interrupted Bobbie, "when I was a kid. There was a man in it and a woman, and you must understand—"

"Got change for half a sovereign?" interrupted the thoughtful youth. "Small silver will do."

"This is all I 'ave," said Bobbie, showing the coins which were left to him, "besides the bob I've got in me hand."

"Ah," said the youth regretfully. "That's no use to me. Put it back in your breast pocket—so. Allow me. If you place your handkerchief over it in this way, you'll find yourself quite safe from thieves."

"I s'pose there are some about still."

"Town's full of 'em," said the other regretfully.

The narrow crowd made a movement, and the pairs closed up. A facetious man in the very front rapped twice at the doors, affecting to be the post.

"What's to-night?" asked the youth suddenly. Bobbie gave the information. "Heavens!" exclaimed the youth, with great concern. "Here am I wasting my time hanging about when I've got an engagement with a lady of title at a reunion."

"Say you forgot all about it," suggested Bobbie.

"I would," said the troubled youth confidentially, "only Lady B.'s such a jealous woman. It's as much as she'll do to let me out of her sight."

"Well," remarked Bobbie, chaffingly, "if you will get mixed up with the fair sex, you must put up with the consequences." The youth went off as the doors opened, and the short, eel-like crowd slipping in demurely, went up the stairs.

When they were all seated it appeared that there was plenty of room for everybody; indeed only the two front rows secured any patrons, and the programme girl at the back, looking down at the scantily filled benches, said something so bitter and satirical to the policeman on duty, that one of her hairpins fell out, and tripped down the steps of the silent gallery, quite startling the few demure people. The patrons spoke in whispers; when Bobbie commenced to whistle, with a view of cheering them, they said "Hush!" and frowned at him.

A few people strayed into the dress circle and into the stalls below; the gentlemen declining to buy programmes, and the ladies pinning their tweed caps to their petticoats. Bobbie called out very loudly, "Orders!" and the constable up at the back interrupted his conversation with the satirical programme girl to whisper a reproof. An important-looking gentleman in white waistcoat came into a box, and surveyed through his opera glasses the gallery with contemptuous air; Bobbie, chafing under this deliberate inspection, and disregarding the indignant looks of his neighbours, said distinctly and repeatedly,—

"Take off that—white—weskit. Take off—that—white—weskit. Take off—that—white—"

Until the important gentleman had to retire defeated behind the hangings of the box. Presently a small orchestra stumbled shyly in, with a conductor, who, having looked round and yawned openly at the house, led them through a sleepy waltz, that eventually induced Bobbie to kick loudly at the wooden front of the gallery. The curtain went up to a few bars of a comic song, and then Bobbie, hopeful of enjoyment, took off his frock-coat, and leaned forward expectantly.

The bills described the play as a highly diverting original comedy fantasy, which was so long a title that it might well have included some of the elements of truth; but, as it proved, did not. A smart young maid and a mild footman were discovered on the stage, and these dusting at nothing in the elaborate breakfast-room with great energy, explained to each other that master had not been home the previous night, that mistress had gone to meet her aunt at Southampton, that this was a rum household, upon their word, and that they would be glad when they should have made enough money to take that little public-house on which they had set their hearts. Nevertheless, the maid boxed the ears of the mild footman soundly when he attempted to kiss her, at which moment one of the many doors in the room opened, and a wild-eyed young man appeared in evening dress, his necktie awry, and a hunted, affrighted look on his face. The two servants having taken his hoarsely-whispered commands for breakfast and disappeared, the distraught-looking master, advancing to the footlights, told the nearly empty house the story of his trouble. Taking advantage, it seemed, of his wife's absence, he had been to a fancy dress ball the night before. There he had met an exceedingly handsome, opulent lady of South American extraction, who comported herself with great hauteur and coldness until a sudden alarm of "Fire" took place; on the instant he had clung to her from sheer nervousness and she had dragged him safely from the place. Arrived outside, the lady, to his amazement, declared him to be her preserver, disclosed her Christian name as Evangeline; swore never to leave him, but to confer upon him her hand in marriage, and when he attempted to fly, ran after him. The smart maid here interrupted, announcing, "A lady to see you, sir, and please mistress has arrived." Entrance of a veiled lady, who, as the young master took refuge under a table, went across and through a doorway; entrance at that instant of young wife; ingenious but inexact explanation of his appearance by the husband; sudden return of the strange lady, who, giving up the veil, cried, "My preserver!" the young husband cried, "My Evangeline!" the young wife cried, "My aunt!" and—curtain on the first act.

"Well," said Bobbie, looking around, "of all the dam silly plays—Ello! Ello! Who's pinched my oof?"

"What say, little boy?"

"Who's took my money," demanded the boy, his face white. He looked under the seat, but it had not fallen out of the pocket. "Three or four bob I had and every penny's gone."

He turned savagely to the lady next him, "Have you got it?"

So far from having Bobbie's money, it appeared that the lady herself had lost a purse which she had carried, for the better convenience of the thoughtful young man outside with the travelling rug, in a back pocket which everybody could get at but herself. Bobbie, sick and depressed at his loss, sat through the rest of the play trying to think out a plan of action, arriving just before eleven at a decision. The husband of the lady who had been robbed of her purse became so elated and triumphant over the event (having, it seemed, always prophesied that this would happen, and being one not often successful in forecasts) that he gave Bobbie sixpence, and Bobbie, after groaning in an unearthly way at the close of the piece, went out and down the stairs into the bright, crowded, busy street, with this coin for only monetary possession.

Charing Cross Station was filled with theatre patrons who, judging from their pleased faces, had been more fortunate than Bobbie, and were now hastening to suburban homes. Ladies in gossamer cloaks flew about excitedly in search of their platform; men in evening dress imperilled the catching of their last train by making frantic rushes to the refreshment bar. Bobbie discovered that the last train to Paddock Wood had gone; discovered also the platform from which the Tonbridge train (Tonbridge being the next convenient station) started, and, taking advantage of a sudden rush at the barrier, slipped in between the people and was borne by them along the platform. There he found the train waiting; found the guard's van of the train; found a corner in the van, and whilst the young guard collected the offertory from third-class passengers for whom he had found room in another class of carriage, Bobbie secreted himself behind a big square wicker basket. The young guard whistled; the engine whistled, the doors banged to, the young guard jumped neatly into his brake, shouting good-night to the officials on the platform; the train went out across the bridge, and presently, after one or two stops, away into the dark country. The boy, crouching uncomfortably in ambuscade, consoled himself with anticipation. Once in the Duchess's hotel comfort and he would not again separate. Perhaps they would put him in a uniform and make him General Commanding of the Hall; he could see the hall lined with giant palms; polite waiters at the far end guarding entrance to an elaborately-furnished dining-room. There would be mirrors with (he felt sure of this) roses painted upon them. He could imagine all this; what he could not adequately picture was the elaborate hot breakfast which the Duchess would cause to be prepared for him.

"And now," said the young guard, entering the van from his compartment, "now for a struggle."

Bobbie, hiding low behind the square basket, trembled. He had some thought of giving himself up and throwing himself upon the mercy of the guard, but he decided to wait. He could hear the rustling of pages as the young guard standing under the roof lamp commenced in a loud voice to recite:—

"A signalman sat in his signal-box
A thinking of this and that,
When the eight-ten mail went rushing by,
And he started, for—"

The young guard made his way steadily through the verses, then closing the book, tried to recite them without assistance, and partly succeeded, partly failed.

"I shall be no more better perfect by Thursday," said the young guard hopelessly, "than my old lamp."

At Tonbridge, when the train stopped—the hour being now near upon one—Bobbie, who had been dozing under the effects of the guard's recital, warily bestirred himself. He waited until the guard had stepped out, and then, by rushing into the centre compartment of the van, he just managed to elude the porters who had thrown open the doors to clear out parcels. Bobbie jumped down from the off side of the brake on to the ballast, and intuitively made his way down the line. He had to reach the next station, Paddock Wood, and then the course would be clear; in all he guessed there was about a ten miles walk before him, and, by refraining from hurry, this ought to take him through the night. He walked carefully away from the station into the black night by the side of the lines, but not so carefully as to avoid an occasional stumble over iron rods connecting the points. By good chance he chose the line which would take him to Paddock Wood, and he made his way stolidly in the darkness along the straight rails, the cornet in his tail pocket knocking at his ankles. Looking back he saw the red and green lights of the junction that he had left; looking forward he saw nothing. Now and again he struck a match for the sake of company, and then for a moment he caught sight of the four shining rails and the tall gaunt telegraph posts; resting at one or two of these posts, he had a talk with them, and listened to their ceaseless humming. He was not afraid yet, because a spirit of adventure was in the air; he knew several boys at the Homes who would have shrieked with terror to find themselves alone like this on a black night in a lonely country with which they were not acquainted. The dead silence was just beginning to terrify him when far ahead he saw two small white eyes. They came nearer and nearer and larger and larger. The boy became nervous. He stopped and stumbled down into the dry ditch that ran along by the side of the railway; the two white eyes came upon him with a hissing sound, Bobbie put his hands over his face and held his breath. A fierce tumultuous rush past; a flash of light. Bobbie venturing to remove his hands after a full minute, saw that the engine, out alone at a time of night when all respectable engines should have been abed, was a distance off, its rear light showing redly.

He felt shaken by this, but he made his way doggedly along the loose ballasted walk, through the dark, still night, trying not to think of what he was doing; nevertheless, he still counted the gaunt telegraph posts, and told each of them its number. He had been walking, he thought, about an hour and a half, when he saw specks of coloured lights in the distance, and he knew that he was nearing a station. From thence he would have to branch off to the right.

"I'm getting on a fair treat," he said, cheerfully.

At Paddock Wood, noise and commotion that were grateful after the silence of the walk. Goods trains blundering about in sidings and excited men with lamps begging them to be reasonable, but the trucks of goods trains declining to listen to advice, and quarrelling and nudging and punching and shoving each other in a great state of ill-temper. Engines, on the earnest appeal of the men with lamps, hurried to restore order, and the occasion being one demanding drastic remedy, half a dozen specially quarrelsome trucks were selected for punishment, a masterful engine drew them out on a middle line, and when one of the men with lamps had uncoupled them, the engine made a sudden rush and sent them all flying away into a distant siding where they could no longer interfere with the general order. Something of quiet ensuing upon this, the engine-drivers drank hot tea out of tin cans, and the shunters with lamps made a hasty meal of thick bread and thick bacon—a meal interrupted by the arrival of a long, overgrown goods train, which insisted upon ridding itself of a dozen trucks, and went after a while with an exultant shriek at having got the best of somebody. Bobbie stood away from all this, watching it with great delight. He had begun to feel sleepy. This awakened him.

He went out through the flat, silent, straggling village, and found, by climbing a finger-post and striking a match, the direction that he had to take for Brenchley. There was a vague touch of lightness now in the starless sky; passing by the quick-set hedge, bordering a churchyard, he could see upright tombstones, dimly white, and the sight depressed the boy, for he knew that here were those whose memory to some was dear. The boy came to cross roads, and then found that his box of matches had disappeared through a hole in his frock-coat pocket. He sat down with his back against the post fixed in the grass triangle at the centre of the roads; before he had time to warn himself to keep awake, his eyes closed. He slept.

"Now, then!" said a voice. "Time all boys was out of bed."

"It's all right, mother," said the boy sleepily. "I was just getting—"

He rubbed his eyes and looked around. Instead of the neat room with its red-counterpaned beds, and the mother of Collingwood Cottage shaking his shoulder—broad daylight and the open country. The person who had awakened him was a uniformed man, with a straight-peaked cap which bore the figure of a horse.

"Know where you are?" asked the uniformed man.

"Just beginning to guess," said the boy blinking.

"Where you bound for?"

"What's it got to do with you?" asked Bobbie, yawning.

"It's got all to do with me, as it happens. I'm the constable in charge of this district."

"Ho, yes!" said the boy incredulously. "Where's your 'elmet?"

"Ah!" remarked the constable, with tolerance. "You're town bred, I can see. What you got in your tail pocket?"

"Cornet."

"Whose?"

"Mine," said the boy defiantly. "Who's did you think?"

"One minute," said the constable sharply. "Haven't done with you yet, my lad. If that's your cornet, and you've come by it honest, you can no doubt play a tune on it."

"Why should I play a tune to an amateur, 'alf-baked copper like you?"

"I've got you," said the constable gleefully. "I've got you, my lad, on a piece of string. Wandering about with no vis'ble means of subsistence; also in possession of property that he is unable to account for. I'll borrow a dog-cart, and take you off to Tonbridge."

"Give it a name, then," said the boy sulkily.

"'Dreamt I dwelt in marble 'alls,'" suggested the constable.

Bobbie played this, and the constable, much delighted, not only gave up all idea of the dog-cart and Tonbridge, but asked for another verse.

"What time do you make it?" asked Bobbie, wiping his lips.

He felt hungry; the thought of hot coffee and hot rolls, and broiled ham and eggs, waiting for him at the Duchess's magnificent hotel, made him anxious. The constable lifted a huge watch from his trousers pocket. "Wants a quarter to six," he said.

"'Appen to know a place up at Brenchley called 'The Happy Retreat'?"

"Do I not."

"Rather fine hotel, isn't it? One of the most important places of its kind in the district, eh?"

"Of its kind," said the constable, "yes."

"Do an extr'ordinary business there, don't they?"

"Most extr'ordinary."

"Which road do I take to get to it quickest?" The constable pointed with his stick. "I know the landlord and the landlady, and I want to get there for breakfast."

"I could see you was well connected," remarked the constable pleasantly, "by the fit of your coat. Give my regards to 'em, and tell 'em from me that ten o'clock's their time for closing, not 'alf-past."

"Right," said Bobbie.

"Give us another verse of 'Dreamt I dwelt,'" begged the constable, "'fore you go."

The country was already rousing itself, being a country that went to bed early, and able, therefore, to rise betimes. Smoke puffed straight out of the chimneys stuck atop of the infrequent cottages; a grateful scent of boiling tea came from the open doors across the gardens of flowers to the roadway. Conceited poultry strutted out to the gate and crowed; birds up in the trees whistled and chirruped ceaselessly; rooks flew about near a row of tall poplars trying their voices, voices which seemed rather hoarse and out of practice. At one place by the side of the roadway where the green border was spacious, gipsies in their yellow-painted van were bestirring themselves, and scantily-clothed, brown-skinned children affected to wash at the brook whilst their parents quarrelled loudly. The male parent broke off to call to Bobbie, asking him if he wanted a lift to London. Bobbie shook his head, and hurried on up the hill. A postman went by on his tricycle, reading the postcards entrusted to him as he went; at the diamond-patterned windows on the top floor of cottages, apple-cheeked, white-shouldered girls were doing their hair, holding a rope of it between their teeth and plaiting the rest. A tramp who had been sleeping in a barn slouched along, picking straws from his deplorable clothes and swearing softly to himself. Men in thick, earth-covered boots came out of their houses to go to their work in the fields, and small babies waved hands to them from the protected doorways. Bobbie noticed, away from the road, a small, dilapidated house with a vague, unintelligible sign-post, and anxious to arrive at the Duchess's hotel without error, he went to inquire. He pushed open the door; stepped in on the floor of uneven bricks. A lazy smell of stale beer pervaded the low-ceilinged passage; to the right was a room with a dirty table, dirtier by reason of sticky rings made by pots of beer. At the end of the table, smooth spaces caused by practice of the game of shove-halfpenny.

"Shop!" called Bobbie.

No answer! He went through the passage. It was a beer-house evidently; a few casks stood about and unwashed earthenware mugs lined the counter. Dirt and untidiness everywhere. Upstairs he heard a voice crooning, and he listened anxiously, for the song seemed familiar.

"You should see us in our landor when we're drivin' in the Row,
You should 'ear us chaff the dukes and belted earls.
We're daughters of nobility—"

"The Duchess!" cried the boy.

The song stopped. A window of the room above opened and the Duchess's voice could be heard upbraiding Mr. Leigh.

"Fat lot of good you do pottering about in the garden and pretendin' you was born and bred in the country. Wish to goodness we was back in Ely Place again."

Mr. Leigh begged that the Duchess would hold her row and let him get on with his scarlet runners in peace.

"Peace?" cried the Duchess, scornfully. "There's a jolly sight too much peace about this dead and alive 'ole. I'm a woman used to a certain amount of seeciety."

Mr. Leigh advised her to go downstairs and have a drop of beer and then get back to bed again.

"Beer and bed," complained the Duchess with great contempt. "That's about all there is in this place. I'd rather be Bat Miller and—"

"For goodness sake," begged Mr. Leigh, "'ush."

"Shan't 'ush," declared the Duchess, preparing to slam the window. "I shall tell everybody why we're come 'ere and what you—"

Mr. Leigh, speaking for once with decision, said imperatively, "Shut that winder and shut your mouth, or else I'll come and do both."

The Duchess obeyed, and Bobbie stood back as he heard her coming in slippered feet down the stairs. Few of us look our best at six o'clock in the morning, and the Duchess formed no exception. It was not easy to glance at her without a shudder.

The boy turned and hurried out. He ran swiftly, crying as he went, down the hill to the gipsies' van.

CHAPTER X

Myddleton West still lived in the rooms over a fancy wool shop in Fetter Lane, which he had rented when he first came to London. At times he had thought of going into one of the Inns close by, and had inspected chambers there, but he found so many ghosts on every landing that, although a man of fair courage, he became affrighted. Over the fancy wool shop in Fetter Lane, no shadows interfered. The Misses Langley kept his rooms carefully dusted, seeing that the panel photograph of an attractive young nurse, with a thoughtful face, never moved from its position of honour on the mantelpiece. Myddleton West was getting on in the world and earning agreeable cheques every month; like many young men in this position, he found it difficult to increase his expenses without taking inordinate pains. Consequently he gave up attempts in this direction, and remained in Fetter Lane, writing early and late on any subject that the world offered, finding this the only way to keep his mind from the thoughtful young woman of the panel portrait. Rarely she took brief holiday from the ward of which she was sister, and they met by appointment at an aerated bread shop, where, over chocolate, she knitted her pretty forehead and talked with the concentrated wisdom of at least three hundred young women, on Myddleton West becoming urgent in his protestations of love, reproving him with a quaint air of austerity that at once annoyed and delighted him. He found no argument in favour of their marriage that she did not instantly defeat by a proud reference to the work which Fate had assigned to her. This was their only contentious subject; once free of it they were on excellent terms, and West took her on from the tea-rooms to private views and to afternoon performances at the theatre, and to concerts, and was an enchanted man until the moment came for her to fly back in her grey silk cloak to the hospital.

"Hullo!" said Myddleton West.

"Excuse me interrupting, sir, in your writing work."

"Doesn't matter, Miss Langley."

"As I often say to my sister," persisted the thin lady at the doorway, "no one can possibly write sense if they're to be continually broken in on—if I may use the expression—and—"

"Somebody called to see me?" asked West, patiently.

"And badgered out of their life," concluded the lady. "I'm sure writing must be quite sufficient a tax on the brains without—"

"Miss Langley."

"Sir to you."

"Do I understand that some one has called to see me?"

"Mr. West," confessed Miss Langley, with a burst of frankness, "some one has called to see you."

"Then," said Myddleton West, definitely, "show them up."

"It isn't a them, sir, it's only a bit of a lad."

"Very well, show him up."

West finished the sentence which he had commenced, and then, hearing a slipping footstep, swung round in his chair again. A boy in a long worn frock-coat, his bowler hat dented, stood at the doorway, white of face, his under lip not quite under control.

"Wha' cheer?" said the boy with an effort to appear at ease. "How goes it with you?"

"Wait a bit," said Myddleton West, rising and standing in front of the fireplace. "Let me see now if I can remember you. Take off your hat." West dropped his pince-nez and peered across the room at the boy. "I'll have three shots," he said presently. "Your name is Cumberland."

"Not a bit like it."

"I met you—let me see—at an inquest in Hoxton some years ago; I saw you later at the police station."

"You're getting warmer. Now try the letter L."

"And your name is Lincoln."

"Bit more to the left."

"Lancaster!"

"A bull's-eye!" said the white-faced boy approvingly. "What'll you 'ave, cigar or a cokernut?" He staggered a little and caught the back of the chair.

"Hungry?" asked West sharply.

"You are a good guesser," replied Bobbie, slipping to the chair. "I 'aven't had a thing to eat for—for a day and a half."

Myddleton West snatched a serviette from the drawer and spread it on the table in front of the boy. In another moment half a loaf of bread, a knuckle of ham, and cheese were on the serviette; in much less than another moment Bobbie had commenced.

"Excuse me wolfin' me food," said the boy with his mouth full. "Don't suppose you know what it is to be famishing. I've had rather rough times the last few days."

"But you went to the Poor Law schools surely. Did you run away?"

"Yes," said Bobbie ruefully. "And I wish now I hadn't. Can I trouble you for a glass of water, sir?"

"Like some lemonade?" asked Myddleton West.

"So long as it's moist, sir, and there's plenty of it, I don't mind what it is."

"And you're not getting on well as an independent man?"

"I'm getting on," said Bobbie, holding up the glass with a trembling hand, "pretty awful." He drank and smacked his lips appreciatively, "Ah!" he said, "that's something like!"

"Eat slowly."

"Does it matter if I finish the bread, sir?"

"I shall be disappointed if you don't."

"Then rather'n cause you any annoyance," said Bobbie with reviving spirits, "I'll undertake to clear it all up."

The meal finished, the boy asked for a cigarette, and, smoking this with great enjoyment, told Myddleton West his adventures. The journey back from Brenchley had not been without drawbacks. At Orpington, Bobbie had interfered on behalf of the gipsy's wife, with the perfectly natural result that she had turned on him indignantly, and both man and wife had, in turns, thrashed him, and had then started him adrift without his cornet. From Orpington to London he had walked.

"And now," said Bobbie—"and now my difficulty is how to get back to the 'omes without looking a silly fool. What would you advise, sir?"

"I should send a wire," counselled Myddleton West promptly. "Apologize for your absence, and say that you will be there in a few hours."

"It'd pave the way a bit," acknowledged the boy.

"Here's a form. Write the address of the Superintendent."

"You must tell us what else to say."

The telegram drawn up on the dictation of the newspaper man, seemed to Bobbie an admirable document; one calculated to remove difficulties. Miss Langley being summoned, the boy was conveyed to the kitchen downstairs, where, furnished with a cake of yellow soap, he remained under the tap for about ten minutes. This so much improved his appearance that when Myddleton West started with him to take train at Blackfriars, the two sisters forced upon his acceptance a triangular chunk of seed cake and a gay almanack with a portrait of the Princess of Wales, which Bobbie decided to take as a propitiatory offering to the mother of Collingwood Cottage. The telegram was despatched from an office in Fleet Street after Bobbie had read it through once more with increased satisfaction.

"It ain't too humble," he said approvingly, "and it ain't too much the other way. Seems to me to hit the 'appy medium."

The fares from Temple Station to Bishopsgate and from Liverpool Street to the destination being ascertained from a railway time book, Bobbie agreed to accept from Myddleton West the precise amount and no more. He showed gratitude with less reserve than he would have exhibited in the years before he entered the Homes, and, as he trotted beside the long-legged journalist, he endeavoured politely to find a subject for conversation that would be pleasing to his companion.

"How are you getting along with your young lady, sir?" he asked with interest.

"No progress," replied West.

"You don't go the right way to work," said Bobbie knowingly. "Women folk can be managed if you only exercise a bit of what I call ingenuity."

"I am always willing, Master Lancaster, to listen to the voice of experience."

"What you want to do," said the young sage, changing step as they went down Arundel Street, "is to be artful without lettin' 'em see that you're artful."

"I know of no plan," said West, "by which, under modern conditions, you can force a lady to marry you if she has decided not to do so."

"Pretend there's another lady," suggested Bobbie;

"Always a risk that the announcement may be received with undisguised satisfaction."

"Can but give it a trial," urged Bobbie. "If she's an ordinary sort of young lady, strikes me she'll marry you like a shot. Is this my station?"

"This is the Temple Station," said West. "Buy your ticket and be careful not to get out of the train before you get to Bishopsgate."

"All right," said Bobbie. "I'm old enough to take care of meself."

"Let me know that you get down safely."

"I shall be as right as rain now. I feel like twenty shillings in the pound since I saw you, sir."

"Good-bye," said Myddleton West, holding out his hand, "and good luck to you."

"Good-bye," said Bobbie, taking the hand awkwardly, "and good luck to you, sir. You know what I mean. And I'm—I'm very much obliged for all your—"

"There's a train coming," interrupted West. "Down you go."

Bobbie, seated near the window of the impetuous underground train, held tightly the large card intender for the mother of Collingwood Cottage, and as he read advertisements in the compartment congratulated himself on the change of circumstances that had come to him within the last hour. He felt grateful for this, and decided that once safely back in the homes and enjoying the sunshine of favour again, he would comport himself in a manner that would be gratifying to those who wished him well. The bitter days of the journey up from Brenchley had proved to him that the world was full of unforeseen and highly inconvenient rocks for a boy who had no one to pilot him; he must wait until he became older before he courted the responsibility of taking charge of himself. In less than an hour he would be through the gates of the Homes; the delicate matter of his return would be all over, and the past few days could be sponged from memory. So far as concerned the underground railway there could be no complaint of delay, for the train seemed in a great hurry to get round the circle, stopping momentarily at one or two stations in a breathless, panting manner, as who should say, Oh, for goodness sake, don't stop me, I'm behind-hand as it is, some other time I'll come round and stay, but just now really—

Other passengers in the compartment went out at one of the stations, and Bobbie stood up at the open window as the train hurried through the black smoky tunnel. The train pulled up, gasping, at another station, starting again immediately with a rough jerk that knocked the card out of Bobbie's hand on to the platform. He jumped out, picked up the portrait and attempted to re-enter the compartment. The porters shouted,—

"Stan' away from the train there!"

"Stan' away, can't you, stan' away!"

"Whoa! Stop! You'll break the door!"

The train pulled up suddenly in a great state of annoyance. At the end of the platform, where the black tunnel began, the boy had been flung and lay a mere bundle on the platform. The carriage door closed; the train went on into the tunnel ill-temperedly. The entire staff and a few stray passengers surrounded the senseless bundle on the platform.

"Here," said the inspector to one of the porters, "you're a 'first aid' man. See if you can tell what the damage is."

"He's 'urt," said the "first aid" man, with a professional air.

"Yes, yes," remarked the inspector, "we could have all guessed that."

"It's a case for the 'ospital," said the "first aid" man cautiously. "I don't feel justified in trying my 'and at it."

"Then," said the inspector, "fetch the ambulance cart, someone, for the poor little beggar, and let's get him there as quick as possible. We can't have passengers dying about here."

CHAPTER XI

Into a long broad ward with scarlet counterpaned cots, headed against the wall on either side, and a shining floor between, Bobbie Lancaster, after being with ever so much tenderness bathed and combed in a small room, was conveyed, and there he relinquished for a few weeks his identity and became Number Twenty. The young doctor whom he saw when first brought into the hospital had whistled softly, and had murmured the words "compound fracture"; the damaged boy felt glad that the injury was of some importance and likely to attract attention. He woke the morning following his arrival on tea being brought round at five o'clock, to find that his arm, accurately bound up with two small boards, gave him less pain than be had expected. There was an acceptable scent of cleanliness in the ward, helped sternly by the universal scent of carbolic, receiving more joyful volunteer assistance from the bowl of heliotrope on the Sister's table at the centre. Turning his head, Bobbie saw a comfortable fire blazing away not far from him; a fire that made all polished things reflect its flames; saw, too, that some of his neighbours were unable to rise, and had to be fed by the white-aproned nurses going softly to each cot. One or two of the numbers had arched protectors under the bedclothes to keep the sheets from touching their small bodies; Number Twenty-one had a head so fully bandaged that there was not much of his face to be seen but the eyes and the tip of a nose; wherefore he was called by the others "Fifth of November." Bobbie's other immediate neighbour, Number Nineteen, a white-faced boy, lost no time in bragging to the new-comer that he possessed hips about as bad as hips could manage to be.

"Well, Twenty," said the nurse to Bobbie cheerfully. "You going to stay at our hotel for a few weeks?" The nurse was a pleasing round-faced young woman, who signalled the approach of an ironical remark by winking; in the absence of this intimation the ward understood Nurse Crowther to be serious. "All the nobility come here," said Nurse Crowther, deflecting her eyelid, "seem to have given up Homburg and Wiesbaden and places, and to have made up their mind to come to Margaret Ward. Here's Lord Bailey, otherwise known as Nineteen, for instance." The white-faced boy laughed at this personal allusion. "He's given up everything," declared Nurse Crowther. "Dances, receptions, partridge shooting, and I don't know what all, just in order that he should come and spend a few months here with us. Isn't that right, Nineteen?"

"Gawspel!" affirmed little Nineteen, in a whisper.

"It must affect some of the other fashionable resorts," said Nurse Crowther, pursuing the facetious vein. "I'm told that there's nobody at Trouville this year, and as for Switzerland—"

"All the time you're trying to be funny," complained Master Lancaster, "you're letting my milk get cold. Why don't you attend to bisness first?"

"Hope you're not going to be a tiresome boy," said the nurse.

"Wait and see."

"I must bring the Sister to see you presently. You've got a nice open face."

"If I've got an open face I can keep me mouth shut," said Twenty, drinking his milk. "That's more than some of you can."

"Arm pretty comfortable this morning?" asked the nurse, good-temperedly, as she smoothed the scarlet counterpane. "Had a good night's rest? Weren't disturbed by the noise of the traffic, were you? What—"

"One at a time, one at a time," said Twenty crossly. "I can't answer forty thousand blooming questions at once."

"Sit back now, there's a dear, and keep as quiet as you can till the doctors come round."

"What time do they put in an appearance?"

"That, dear duke," said the nurse winking, "entirely depends upon you. You have but to say the word."

"If there's one thing I can't stand more'n another," said the boy, settling himself down cautiously, "it is gels trying to be comic."

The young doctor with three or four men still younger, and all of them endeavouring to look an incalculable age, paid their visit to Margaret Ward in due course, and Bobbie felt indignant because whereas they stayed at the end of his bed but a couple of minutes writing some casual marks on the blue form pinned on the board above his head, at the next bed they ordered a screen to be placed, and behind this they remained in consultation over the white-faced little Nineteen for quite a long time. When they had gone, Bobbie salved his jealousy by telling Nineteen at once that Nineteen need not think himself everybody, giving a long list of imaginary complaints that he (Bobbie) had in the past suffered from, ranging in character from a wart on the knuckles to complete paralysis of the right side.

This seemed to restrain any idea that Nineteen might have had of exhibiting conceit, and that little chap contented himself by offering to bet two to one in halfpennies that he would he the next in the Margaret Ward to go. Bobbie forced the odds to three to one, and then closed with the wager.

"I shan't be sorry," said white-faced Nineteen, "'pon me word I shan't. It can't be much worse than this."

"You be careful how you talk," advised Bobbie. "A man that's getting near to kicking the bucket can't be too cautious of what he says."

"Likely as not," said Nineteen, "it'll he a jolly sight better than this."

"How can you tell?"

"Anyway," said Nineteen, "it'll he a rare old lark to watch and see what 'appens. I 'eard a man arguin' once in Victoria Park that those what put up with a lot in this world, got it all their own way in the next, and vicer verser."

"How did he get to know?"

"Of course," admitted Nineteen, "it's all speculation." Little Nineteen yawned. "I feel bit tired."

"You take jolly good care what you're about, old man," recommended Bobbie. "You'll look jolly silly if you find yourself all at once in 'ell."

"Even that'd be interesting."

"And hot," said Bobbie.

"I shouldn't mind chancing it a bit," said Nineteen, "only there's the old woman. She worries about me a good deal, she does."

"Your mother?"

"She'd he upset if she thought I hadn't gone to 'Eaven." Nineteen gave the skeleton of a laugh. "You know what Primitive Methodists are," he added excusingly.

"Tell you what," said Bobbie. "If anything 'appens to you and you pop off the hooks, I'll tell her that you were going there all right, and I'll make up something about angels, and say they was your last words. See!"

"I shall take it very kind of you," said little Nineteen thankfully.

"You leave it me. And touchin' that bet. Just occurs to me. If you lose you mayn't be able to pay."

"If I win I shan't be able to dror it off of you."

"Never mind," said Bobbie, "we'll see what 'appens."

"I've never stole nothin'," urged Nineteen, after a pause.

"You're all right." With some awkwardness.

"I've never had a copper even speak to me."

"You're as right as ninepence. There's lots of cheps worse than you."

"I've got to 'ave port wine and jellies," remarked Nineteen after a pause.

"Some of you get all the luck," said Bobbie. At which Nineteen dozed off contentedly.

When, later in the morning, the tall young Sister came up to Bobbie's cot and introduced herself, he permitted her to talk for some time, and watched her quiet, attractive face. Dressed in her plain gown, she looked, the boy thought, perfect, and he touched the white hand that rested on the coverlet of his bed with shy respect. Sister Margaret talked of his accident; chatted about the other numbers of the ward. Leaving him for a moment to give white-faced Nineteen a kiss, she was called back by Bobbie.

"I say, Miss."

"Well, Twenty."

"Something to ask you. Bend down."

As the tall young woman obeyed, Bobbie put one hand to his mouth in order that his confidential inquiry might not be heard by the other boys. "How's your young man?" he whispered.

Sister Margaret flushed and stood upright.

"What do you mean, Twenty?" she answered, severely. "You must understand that here we don't allow boys to be impudent."

"It's all right, Miss," whispered Bobbie. "Don't fly all to pieces. I'm not chaffing of you. I mean Mr. West—Mr. Myddleton West."

"You know Mr. West?" she said, bending down again.

"Rather!" said the boy. "Saw your photograph in his place yesterday. Only one in the room."

She sat down beside the bed, her eyes taking a light of interest. Bobbie looking round the ward to see that this special honour was being noted, and observed that the numbers on the opposite side scowled jealously at him.

"I've known him off and on," said Bobbie, "these two or three years. Good sort, he is."

"Mr. West is indeed a very good fellow," said the Sister earnestly. "But you—you are wrong, Twenty, in assuming that we are engaged. Nothing, in point of fact, is further from the truth. We are very good friends, and that is all."

"You don't kid me," said the boy knowingly.

"Twenty! I shall be extremely annoyed if, whilst you are in the ward, you couple my name with Mr. West's."

"Shouldn't think of doing so, Sister," he said seriously. "If there's one thing I can do better than another it is keeping a secret. Once I make up my mind to shut my mouth, wild 'orses wouldn't open it."

"I like him," she went on (it appeared that the Sister was not averse to speaking of Myddleton West), "I like him very much, but it is possible to like a person, Twenty, without going so far as to become engaged."

"Depends!"

"There are several courses open nowadays to women," she said half to herself, and with something of enthusiasm. "It is no longer marriage or nothing for them. There are certain duties in the world—public duties—that a woman can take upon herself, and marriage would only interfere with their performance. The old idea of woman's place in the world was, to my mind, not quite decent. We are getting away from all that, and we are coming to see that the possibilities—"

"Don't he mind your taking up with this nonsense?" asked Bobbie. The boy's interruption stopped the argumentative young woman. She laughed brightly at finding herself lecturing to Twenty on this subject, and, smoothing his pillow before she went, asked him with a smile whether he did not agree with her.

"I call it a silly ass of an idea," he said frankly.

This was not the last talk that he had with the tall young Sister of the ward, and for some days in that week the ward inclined to mutiny on account of the disproportionate time that she gave to Twenty and to little Nineteen. It almost seemed that Nineteen showed signs of improvement under the combined influence of her visits and the companionship of Bobbie his neighbour; Bobbie's predecessor had been a gloomy boy, with his own views in regard to details of eternal torments, and Bobbie's optimism cheered the white-faced boy so much that when his tearful mother came to see him, being by special permission admitted at any time, she found herself debating with him on his walk in life when he should grow up, and discussing the relative advantages of the position of engine-driver as compared with that of policeman. Nineteen introducing his neighbour, Nineteen's mother gave Bobbie two oranges and an illuminated card bearing minatory texts. Bobbie enjoyed the oranges.

"I think he's better, nurse," said Nineteen's mother respectfully. "Seems to have got more colour, and—"

"It's my belief," answered Nurse Crowther at the foot of the bed, "that there's nothing whatever the matter with his lordship. I believe it's all his nonsense. I tell him that he'll have to take me to the theatre some evening, soon as ever he gives up playing this game of lying in bed."

Little Nineteen smiled faintly. The good-humoured nurse went and placed her cool hand on his forehead.

"I don't hold with theatres, nurse," said Nineteen's mother precisely. "To my mind chapel is a great deal better than all these devil's playhouses."

"Dam sight duller," remarked Bobbie.

"Twenty! I'm surprised."

"Well, nurse," said Bobbie excusingly, "she said 'devil.'"

"Anyway," remarked Nurse Crowther, "we're going to dodge off somewhere, the very first day he gets well, aren't we, Nineteen?"

Happy nod of acquiescence from the tired boy.

"And we shan't say anything to anybody else about it, shall we, Nineteen?"

Not a word, signalled poor Nineteen.

"And, goodness! how people will stare when they see us on the steamer together off to Rosherville."

"I'll come with you," interposed Bobbie from the next bed.

"Not likely," declared Nurse Crowther, with another wink. "Two's company, three's a crowd. Aye, Nineteen?"

"Most decidedly," intimated the delighted boy.

"And now it's time for your little pick-me-up. Say good-bye to your mother."

Nineteen's mother, having said good-bye, drew the nurse aside, whispering a question, and Bobbie heard the answer, "No hope!" This startled Bobbie, and made him think; presently he worked so hard in the endeavour to cheer little Nineteen that Sister Margaret had to command silence, because Nineteen required rest. That night, when the ward was silent, Bobbie watched him as he lay with eyes closed, his breathing short and irregular, and for almost the first time in his life, Bobbie thought seriously of the desirability—taking everything into consideration—of becoming religious.

He could see the red fire, and watching it he considered this entirely new suggestion. He lifted the bed-clothes to shield himself from the sight of the distant fireplace, for he was becoming heated. It required much determination to put gloomy thoughts from him; when he had partly succeeded in doing this he looked again at the fire, and then he knew that there were tears in his eyes, because the light of the fire became starry and confused in appearance. He sniffed and rubbed his eyes. It seemed that he could see another fire, a small one, near to the grate, and this he assumed to be an optical delusion until it crept along a black rug and commenced to blaze, whereupon he slipped cautiously out of bed; his bandaged arm paining, despite his care, and called for the nurse. An answer did not come immediately, and the boy hurried bare-footed, in his scarlet gown only, across the floor to the burning rug. Afterwards, he remembered rolling it up awkwardly with one hand and stamping upon it; the night nurse hurrying up with a scream, forty heads up in forty cots—it was then for the first and last time in his life that Bobbie fainted.

"We shall have to send you to a home, Twenty." Sister Margaret looked on a day or two later, whilst Nurse Crowther re-bound the lint and wool. "A convalescent home down by the sea-side, upon a hill, where you can watch the shipping, and—"

"That'll suit me down to the ground, Sister."

"I believe he got burnt purposely, Sister," declared Nurse Crowther, "so that he should have a nice long holiday. Wish to goodness I was half as artful as Twenty is."

"I'm sure," said Sister Margaret sedately, "that Twenty is a very brave boy. If it hadn't been for his courage there might have been quite a serious fire."

Twenty blushed.

"Twenty has qualities," went on the tall Sister, "that if properly directed—I should bring it twice over the knee, nurse, I think—will make him a fine young fellow, and a credit to his country." Sister Margaret had raised her voice in order that her words might be heard. The ward listened alertly; little Nineteen, whose eyelids were now very tired, moving his head in order to hear. "Wrongly directed," she said, lowering her voice, "they will only make him dangerous."

"I should rather like to grow up and—and be brave," said little Nineteen from the next bed.

"So you shall," declared Nurse Crowther, cheerily, "so you shall, Nineteen. If you don't get the Victoria Cross some day, Nineteen, never believe me again." Little Nineteen consoled, closed his eyes wearily. "As for you, Marquis," went on Nurse Crowther, pinning the end of the roll with which Bobbie's limb had been enveloped, "I believe that what Sister says is perfectly true. If you can only keep on the main line you'll make a capital journey. Only don't get branching off."

"If I don't get along in the world," said Bobbie, with a touch of his old impudence, "it won't he for the want of telling."

"You ought to be grateful, my Lord Bishop," said Nurse Crowther, adjusting the bed-clothes carefully, "that you've got so many friends."

"Me!" echoed the boy. "Why, I ain't got a friend in the world."

"Twenty!" said Sister Margaret reprovingly. "And Mr. West is coming all the way down here next visiting day specially to see you."

"To see me?"

"Yes," said Sister Margaret, a little unsteadily, "to see you."

"Reckon," said the boy, looking up, "he's going to kill two birds with one stone. What he's really coming for is to see—"

"Twenty," she commanded, "silence!"

"Is to-morrow visiting day?" asked the thin voice of Nineteen, sleepily.

"To-morrow," replied Nurse Crowther. "And mind you're nice and bright, Saucy Face, by three o'clock against your mother comes."

In the ward the next day occurred the usual excitement that preceded an afternoon for visitors. Little Nineteen alone uninterested; it almost seemed that he had ceased to take concern in worldly matters such as the arrival of apples and other contraband, and to be content, when not asleep, with staring very hard at the ceiling. Bobbie himself, cheered by receipt of a kindly note from Collingwood Cottage, gave his best endeavours to the task of enlivening Nineteen ("Sop me goodness," said Bobbie, reproachfully to himself, "if I ain't getting fond of the little beggar"), but with no result. Elsewhere in the ward movement and expectation; Sister Margaret and the nurses had trouble to preserve sanity amongst the boy patients. Thirty-five declared privately his opinion that all the clocks were slow; that someone had put them back on purpose; Thirty-five added darkly that if he could find the person responsible for the deed he would make it a County Court job. Nevertheless, the hour presently struck, and two minutes afterwards came the sound of many footsteps in the passage; the swing doors opened, and the visitors marched in under the narrow inspection of every scarlet-gowned occupant of every scarlet-counterpaned bed. There were sounds of kissing in different parts of the ward. Bobbie ordered Nineteen to wake up and look sharp about it, but little Nineteen did not answer.

"If you please, Miss, is there a boy named Robert Lancaster in this ward?"

Bobbie's head came up. Nurse Crowther pointed him out to a young girl, dressed quietly, her hair rolled up into a neat bunch, and wearing brown gloves fiercely new. She carried a small paper bag, and looked casually at her silver watch as she advanced to the bedside of Twenty.

"What ho!" said Bobbie, not unkindly. "Who sent for you?"

"Mother told me I might come," said Miss Trixie Bell, breathlessly, "and mother sent this bunch of the best grapes she could get in Spitalfields Market, and mother said I was to give you her kind regards, and tell you to get well as soon as you could."

"Left to meself," said Bobbie, "I should never 'ave thought of that. They ain't so dusty them grapes, though, are they?" he added, admiringly.

"I should rather think not," said Trixie. "They cost money. How's your arm? You look nice and neat in your scarlet—" Miss Bell checked herself and bit her lips. "I nearly said bed-gown," she remarked, apologetically, taking out her watch again.

"You've altered," said Bobbie, "since you came to see me last."

"Mother says I'm going to grow up tall."

"Take care you don't grow up silly the same time. Where'd you get your watch from?"

"Fancy your noticing," said Trixie Bell, delightedly. "That's new to-day. Mother gave it me because it was my birthday, and I'd helped nicely with the shop."

"Many 'appy returns," he said, gruffly.

"Thank you, Bobbie."

"Ever see anything of them Drysdale Street bounders? I mean Nose and Libbis and—"

"I never take no notice of nobody," said the young lady, precisely. "Mother says its best to ignore them altogether. Mother says its unwise even to pass the time of day. So when they call out after me, I simply walk on as though I hadn't 'eard."

"That's right," said Bobbie, approvingly.

"Your neighbour's asleep."

"Little beggar's always at it. He'll wake up directly when his mother comes."

A scent of flowers and a familiar deep voice. Trixie, who had been resting one elbow on the pillow, drew back, as Myddleton West came up.

"Well, young man," said Myddleton West, cheerily, "how are we getting on? Sister Margaret has been telling me of your fire brigade exploit."

"That was nothing."

"It might have been, apparently, if you had not acted as you did. This a friend of yours?" Miss Bell stood up and bowed. "Why, I've met you two together before. On a tram going Shoreditch way on the night when—"

"Let bygones be bygones," said Bobbie, uneasily. "That was ages ago."

"When you were mere boy and girl?"

"Jesso!"

"Sister Margaret thinks of getting you away to a convalescent home," said Myddleton West.

"You seem to have had a rare old chat with her," said the boy, pointedly. "Give her them flowers, instead of leaving them here. They'll please her."

"Excuse me," interrupted Trixie, "don't you think you ought to call the nurse for this little chap in the next bed? I've just touched his hand, and somehow—"

Nurse Crowther and another nurse come quickly to the bed of Nineteen. Nurse Crowther flies for the screen; when this is fixed around the bed, a doctor is sent for. The doctor hurries in, goes away directly, but the screen remains. Nineteen's mother arriving tardily with oranges for her boy, is admitted behind the screen, and there comes presently the sound of weeping.

"Ain't he woke up, Nurse?" asks Bobbie, anxiously.

"Nearly time for visitors to go," says Nurse Crowther. "You'll soon have to say good-bye. Nice bright day outside, they tell me."

"Ain't he woke up yet, Nurse?"

"Who, your Highness?"

"Why, Nineteen."

For once Nurse Crowther's wink declines to respond to her summons. Her lips move, and she puts her hand up to control them.

"My chick," she says, "Nineteen won't wake again in this world." The bed clothes go quickly over Bobbie's head, and remain there for some few minutes. When Sister Margaret's voice is heard warning visitors of the approach of half-past four, his head reappears rather shamefacedly.

"Trixie."

"Yes, Bobbie."

"Anybody looking?"

"Not a soul."

"Well," whispers Bobbie, "if you like to bend down, you can give me a kiss."

Miss Bell takes sedate advantage of this offer, and, readjusting her hat, when she has done so, finds her bright brown gloves.

"Thank you, Bobbie," says Miss Bell. Then she adds very softly, "Dear."

"Not so much of the 'dear,'" orders Bobbie.


CHAPTER XII

The seaside institution to which Bobbie, with an attention that could not have been exceeded if he had been paying money recklessly to everybody around him, found himself conveyed, exactly fitted his desires. The cool, calm order of the place, the quiet service of serene women attendants in their dark gowns and white aprons, the well-chosen table, the pure white linen in spotless bedrooms—all these things, that might have irritated the boy had he been perfectly well, were, in his convalescent state, precisely what he required. The days had become warmer, and it was possible to spend a good deal of time on the wooden balconies of the Swiss-like building. From these balconies he could look away across the green waters, with their patches of dark purple; could watch the Channel steamer puffing its way across, presently to enter the harbour below. The harbour itself never ceased to delight him. There it was that steamers rested in a dignified manner when off duty, submitting themselves to an energetic washing of decks and rubbing of brasswork; near them, brown-sailed fishing vessels for ever going out to sea or coming back from sea, manned by limited crews, who shouted in the dialect of the Kentish coast, and whose aim in life it appeared to be not so much to do work themselves as to tell others to do it. The scent of the sea came up to the balconies, and most of the boys in varying stages of repair who inhaled it, declared their intention, once they had regained possession of that health which for the moment eluded them, of becoming admirals in her Majesty's navy. Bobbie Lancaster on this subject said nothing, which was his way when engaged in making up his mind.

Stages marked the progress of improvement. One of the earliest came on permission being granted to walk about the green-grassed lawn around the Home, with its summer-houses, where, over the fence in the evenings, you could observe sons of mariners wooing, with economic speech, daughters of other mariners, and kissing them, under the impression that no one but a Martello tower looked on.

Here Bobbie himself fell in love.

A breezy curate attached to the church close by, for ever flying in and out of the Home with no hat, and an appearance of having another engagement of a highly urgent character for which he was a little late, hurried in one day to look round the sitting-room where the guests played dominoes, and found Bobbie well enough to go out; so well, indeed, that he had arranged to go down the long road towards the white cliffs in company with an adult patient, who, being in ordinary times a stoker on a London Bridge and Greenwich steamboat, posed as authority on all matters concerning the navy, and arbitrator in disputes concerning that branch of the service. Breezy Curate, in less than no time at all, found other work for the naval authority, gained the necessary permission from the Lady Superintendent, and was away with Bobbie, walking so fast that he had to run back now and then in the manner of a frisky terrier, in order that Bobbie should keep up with him. Ere the boy had time or breath to ask questions they arrived at the door of a round squat Martello tower (called by elderly acquaintances Billy Pitt's Mansion), where he was lugged in and introduced to the coastguardsman who lived there; introduced also to coastguardsman's immense niece, who appeared to Bobbie, panting on a chair, like a very large angel, only better dressed and much better looking, and who, it appeared, came in daily to make tidy her uncle's tower. Breezy Curate, before hastening off for a fly along the cliffs, made the boy a friend of Coastguard and Coastguard's niece, and promised to call back for him in an hour.

"Reckon you've been 'avin' games, young man, ain't you?" said Coastguard sternly. "What made you fall down and step on yerself in that manner for, eh?"

Bobbie explained. When he described the fire in Margaret Ward, the large angel, making tea and toasting bread that filled the small room with most appetizing odours, looked up.

"Bravo," said the young woman. "Come here and I'll give ye a kiss for that."

Bobbie hesitated.

"Go on, lad," counselled her uncle; "there's them that wouldn't want to be asked twice to do that, jigger me if they would."

"Uncle!" said the large angel reprovingly. "Do give over."

Bobbie considered it proof of the young woman's angelic nature that, seeing he did not stir, she came to him, toasting-fork in hand, gave him a hug and then went back to her work at the fire. Coastguard, enormously amused at this, slapped his knee, saying that seeing kisses were cheap, jigger him if he wouldn't have one, and a kiss he therefore took, and the three sat down to tea in great good-humour. By an effort, Bobbie determined to retain the correct behaviour that he had learnt in the Cottage Homes and at Margaret Ward; Coastguard, delighted with the boy's respectful manner, declared that an earl could not comport himself better. From this, Coastguard passed, by easy transition, to a review of the Royal Family of his country, a review that became a glowing eulogy. The angel, too, preparing to cut cake, expressed so much affection for the younger members of the family, portraits of whom were on the walls of the little room of the Martello tower, that the boy found himself impressed, and convinced by views in regard to Royalty that were novel to him.

"Old Lady," declared Coastguard, blowing at his tea, "will have the best. She don't mind what she pays for her Navy, but she will 'ave it good."

"I see what you mean," said Bobbie.

"Do you like the outside or the inside?" asked the angel at the cake.

"Both, Miss," said Bobbie.

"None of your ne'er-do-wells for her," went on Coastguard. "None of your thieving—"

"You've dropped your knife on the floor, little boy," said the angel. "That's a sign you're not careful."

"'None of your bad characters, none of your criminals for my Navy,' she ses, 'if you please.' And jigger me," said Coastguard explosively, "jigger me if the old Lady ain't right."

"You ought to call her 'Her Majesty,' uncle. You'd look silly if she happened to be listening."

"Go' bless my soul," said Coastguard with enthusiasm, "she wouldn't mind it from me. She knows my way of talking."

"And," stammered Bobbie, "is it—is it true then that you can't get into the Navy if you've done anything wrong?"

"Devil a bit," answered Coastguard. "Old Lady'd think it was a piece of impudence to try it on. Looey, my gell, whilst I'm havin' my pipe jest give us a toon on the old harmonium."

The large niece, seated at the harmonium, seemed, to the thoughtful Bobbie, more like an angel than ever; the music she produced helped to distract his troubled thoughts. Presently, however, the angel found a Moody and Sankey book and, having propped it on the ledge before her, picked out on the keys as with her foot she moved the pedals, a hymn that gave the boy memories. The Coastguard rolled his head to the rhythm; now and again taking his pipe from his mouth to growl a note or two and thus give his niece encouragement.

"Dare to be a Daniel,
Dare to stand alone,

Dare to—"

Bobbie sat forward in his chair, his eyes fixed on the broad bending back of the young lady at the harmonium, and thought of Ely Place. What a long way off Ely Place seemed now; Bat Miller, and Mrs. Bat Miller, and the Fright; all these were misty figures that for years had visited his memory infrequently. Bat Miller's time would be up in a year or two. Bobbie shivered to think what he should do were Bat Miller's face to appear suddenly at the window. For a few moments he dared not glance at the window, fearful that this impossible event might happen; when at the end of the hymn he nerved himself to look in that direction he felt almost surprised to find no face peering in.

"Gi' us," said the Coastguard cheerfully, "Gi' us 'Old the Fort.' That's the one I'm gone on. There's a swing about 'Old the Fort.'"

It seemed to the boy that already he had lived two lives; that the first had been broken off short on the day he turned out of Worship Street Police Court. He could not help feeling a vague admiration for that first boy because the first boy had been a fine young dare-devil, never trammelled by rules of behaviour; at the same time it was as well, perhaps, that the first boy had ceased to live, for he was not the kind of lad Bobbie could have introduced to the angel.

"And now," said the Coastguard, "jigger my eyes if I mustn't on with my jacket and find my spy-glass and see what's going on outside. Where's that young curate got to, I wonder?"

The Coastguard went presently, after telling Bobbie that he might call again at the Martello tower, and that if he behaved he should one day go out to the Coastguard Station and see, by aid of the telescope, the coast of France. Bobbie, alone with the angel, and allowed to seat himself at the end of the harmonium, behaved with a preciseness and a decorum that in any other lad would have been held by Bobbie as good justification for punching that boy's head. The angel's right hand remaining on the higher keys for a space in order to give full effect to a final chord, he bent and kissed it. The scent of brown Windsor soap ever afterwards reminded him of this first essay in affection.

"What ye up to?" demanded the angel.

"Only kissin' your 'and," said Bobbie confusedly.

"We don't kiss hands down in these parts," said the large young lady. "That ain't Kentish fashion."

"I like you," remarked the boy shyly.

"My goodness!" said the angel with affectation of much concern, "this won't do. I mustn't be catched alone with a young man what says things like that. I'd better be seeing about taking you back to the home, I reckon."

The curate not returning (having, as it proved, flown away to a neighbouring parish and forgotten all about the boy), this course had to be adopted, and the two walked back along the road on the edge of the white cliffs—Bobbie in a state of proud ecstasy, which reached its highest point, when a boy, in passing them, called out to him, "Why doan' you marry the girl?" The angel herself spoke of the amount that the starting of a household cost; of the relative advantages of a house with folding doors but no bay windows, compared with a house having bay windows, but no folding doors; all in a manner that seemed to the boy, strutting by her side, highly encouraging, and, under the circumstances, as much as on such brief acquaintance a man could reasonably expect. At the home, any trouble that might have arisen by reason of the boy's extended absence was removed by the fact that the angel had once been a highly-esteemed servant at the Institution; the Lady Superintendent met them without a frown. The large young lady found herself lugged into the kitchen by two of the white-aproned maids for a chat, and when presently she looked in to say good night, at the reading-room where Bobbie was finishing a sea story, she kissed him, to the great envy of the other convalescent young students.

"Serve us all alike, Miss," begged a lad with crutches.

"You be quiet," ordered Bobbie, "unless you want your head punched."

"Give me 'alf a one," urged the lad with crutches.

"No fear," said the angel cheerfully. She nodded her head to Bobbie. "He's my young man."

"Should have thought you'd got better taste, Miss."

"You leave off talking to that lady," growled Bobbie, "or I'll spoil your features for you." The large young lady waved her hand and disappeared through the swing doors. "If you ain't a gentleman, do, for goodness sake, try to 'ide the fact."

In the few weeks of Bobbie's residence, the Coastguard became his very good friend. The boy learned the secrets of flags, listened with an interest that he had never felt at school to the accounts of British victories by sea in the past, absorbing with great appetite the Coastguard's figures illustrating the current state of the Navy. In his young heart patriotism was born.

Permitted to see through the telescope the coast of France, he commenced to realize actualities that he had never gained from maps. In the school of the Cottage Homes the general impression amongst incredulous small boys had been that no such places as foreign countries really existed; that these were fictions invented by adults for the more complete annoyance and trouble of children. Now the line of cliffs where on bright days tiny black specks could be seen moving, brought conviction; the boy found that he had much to learn, and something to forget. One Sunday afternoon, being allowed to go down to the sleeping harbour, and over the line, and along the quay by the Customs House, he met, by happy chance, the angel, in white, with green sunshade, who, it appeared, waited for some one who would be free as soon as the baggage had been cleared; together they watched the Channel steamer bustle in and wake up the harbour, saw ropes thrown, gangways fixed, and presently heard the arriving passengers chattering in a language which the angel told him was French.

"Ignorant set, ain't they?" asked Bobbie.

"Oh, I don't know," said the large young lady tolerantly.

"I 'aven't got much opinion of foreigners," said the boy. "For one thing, why don't they learn a decent language like ourn?"

"I s'pose they get on all right without it."

"Do you know any French?"

"A bit," said the angel modestly.

"Tell us some!"

"Je vous aime," said the angel. On Bobbie demanding a translation, the large young lady, shading her face with the green parasol, furnished this.

"Who learnt it you?" demanded Bobbie jealously.

"Ah," said the angel acutely, "that's tellings."

It galled him considerably on the last occasion that the breezy young curate took him under his wing to fly away with him along the cliff and look in at the Martello tower for a picture of a ship which the Coastguard had promised to him, to find the small room almost wholly occupied by a tall bashful young Customs officer, with limbs so long that when he sat down his knees came up in a manner which Bobbie considered eminently ridiculous. The angel had not arrived, but was expected; when the curate insisted upon Bobbie coming away with him, his picture of the ship under his arm, in order that they might skirt the cliffs swallow-like once more, Bobbie complied with hesitation, being thus denied the joy of seeing the lady of his heart.

"I'd like to stay 'ere all me bloomin' lifetime," said Bobbie to the Lady Superintendent that night.

Nevertheless, the next day he had to listen to the voice of reasonableness, to pack up the books that had been given him by the curate, the picture that Coastguard had presented, and a marvellous four-bladed knife from the angel, for which he had paid to that young lady the sum of one halfpenny, in order that the knife might not, in its keenness, sever friendship. He said good-bye to the Lady Superintendent, remembering (just in time) to say, "Thank you," a phrase with which he had become on intimate terms, and walked stolidly down to the station, where a train would take him back to London and the Homes. As he looked at the contents of the bookstall (he had begun in those days to feel an appetite for reading, and a strange craving when not furnished with something in the form of printed words) to him appeared:—

First, the angel! Bobbie had felt confident that the large young lady would not allow him to depart without giving him an opportunity of formally declaring his love; he had already decided on the form of his address.

Second, the curate! Curate flying in through the booking office, skimming restlessly up and down the platform, chatting with porters, chucking babies under the chin, and telling the station-master how a railway ought to be managed.

Third, Coastguard. Jiggering everything at frequent intervals; handing over to Bobbie as final gifts a parcel of huge ham sandwiches and a model clockwork steamer.

Fourth, as the train signalled from the preceding station, an entirely unnecessary person in the shape of the tall Customs officer, rather shy, but taking up, as it seemed to Bobbie, the unwarrantable attitude of being a friend of the family, and brushing from the angel's brown cape a few specks of dust with a calmness for which Bobbie, circumstances willing, could have felled him to the platform.

"I say," said Bobbie, leaning out of the carriage window, when he had been helped into the train, "I want to speak to you."

"Me?" asked the Customs.

"You?" said Bobbie, with infinite scorn. "Good 'Eavens, no. I mean her." The angel stepped forward. "I want to ask you something," he said rather unsteadily.

"I know what it is," declared the angel gaily. "You want me to remember to send you some of the cake."

"What cake?"

"Oh, as if you didn't know," said the angel reproachfully. "Why, my weddin' cake, of course. Don't say you haven't heard that me and him," indicating the tall Customs officer, "are going to be married next month at—. Now you're off. Good-bye, dear."

"Be a good lad," cried Coastguard, as the train moved.

"Be sure to get out at Cannon Street," called the curate, flying along the platform, "and don't forget to say your prayers at night."

When, two hours later, the train ran into the London terminus, porters surveyed with critical eye each compartment, and having made hurried selections, staked out their claim by seizing a carriage handle as they trotted along till the train stopped. Bobbie, rather ill-tempered on the journey because his affairs of the heart had been so brutally checked, had his head out of the window as the train slowed up.

"Any luggage?" asked the porter breathlessly.

Bobbie shook his head, and the porter hurried on in search of a more encumbered traveller. Bobbie, walking down the crowded platform to the barrier, found the word luggage remaining in his mind. It recalled evenings with Bat Miller at stations on the other side of the City, followed sometimes by an interesting review of the contents of a portmanteau or a lady's dressing-case in Ely Place. Around the guard's van, now disgorging its contents hurriedly and confusedly, passengers stood as though at an auction, and when they saw an article of luggage in tune with their desires, held up a hand, and the article being knocked down to them, they bore it off without further question. In the centre, one of the busy porters acting as auctioneer held up a bright brown portmanteau with initials painted boldly.

"Anybody claim this?" demanded the harried porter. "Anybody claim a bag with—. A bundle of rugs, lady? I'll look after it in 'alf a moment, if you'll only leave off prodding me in the back with that gamp of yours."

"I want," said Bobbie's voice, "a bag marked L. C. E."

"Why," grumbled the porter, handing it over to Bobbie, "'ere 'ave I been the last five minutes trying to find a owner for it? Want a cab?"

"No," said Bobbie, "I'll carry it."

"It's a bit lumpy," remarked the porter warningly.

"I know," said the boy.

He gave up his ticket at the barrier and lugged the heavy bag across to a departure platform.

It was, as the porter had said, a heavy bag, and anxious as the boy felt to get away with it, he found himself obliged to rest for a moment when he had reached the platform. Then he started on again, the heavy portmanteau bumping against his knee. Through his alert little head a scheme had already danced; a scheme necessitating an empty compartment to permit of a selection from the articles which the bag contained, and the disposal of the bag itself. This would have the advantage of deferring the awkward duty of returning to the Cottage Homes that day. A nurse walked by on the platform, with flowing cloak and white bands; Bobbie's mind was recalled to Sister Margaret. From Sister Margaret his thoughts went to his other friends. He sat down on the portmanteau; his breath came quickly.

"They'd all look pretty straight," he said to himself, "if they knew." He rose slowly, and gripped the stout leather handles of the bag. "'Owever, I ain't going to be copped. There's plenty that do a thing like this quietly and never so much as—"

He stopped. Across the line on the wall a large portrait in an advertisement frame had—a cloud of engine smoke disappearing—come into view. Bobbie stared at it.

"The old Lady," he muttered.

The portrait of her Majesty the Queen of England and Great Britain looked across at Bobbie with, as it seemed to him, a look of surprise, mingled with reproof. A train whistled, a ticket collector shouted, "North Kent train to Blackheath," but the boy did not move. When the train had started, and the smoke had cleared away, Bobbie found his attention still held by the portrait on the other platform.

"The old Lady," he quoted, under his breath, "will 'ave the best. She don't mind what she pays for her navy, but she will 'ave it good. None of your criminals for her navy, if you please."

He started up, his face white and perspiring. Lugging the weighty portmanteau back to the arrival barrier, he staggered determinedly through.

"Tell you what," a young officer lad was saying fiercely. "If you porters don't find that fearful bag of mine I'll—"

"'Scuse me," interrupted Bobbie, placing the portmanteau at the feet of its owner. "My mistake. Took it off in the hurry, instead of me own."

"I'm really most fearfully obliged," declared the officer lad effusively. "It has my dress suit, don't you know, and I should have looked such a fearfully silly fool this evening without it."

"You're saved from that now, sir," said the inspector, pointedly.

"What I mean to say is, I'm so fearfully indebted to you that really—"

"Don't name it," said Bobbie. "Glad I brought it back in time."

"Good-bye, old chap," said the officer lad, shaking hands with the boy. "I'm most fearfully glad to have met you. Can't give you a lift, I suppose, anywhere, can I, what?"

"Thanks, fearfully," said Bobbie. "My brougham's waiting outside for me. Ta-ta!"


## CHAPTER XIII

Roses at Collingwood upon his return; and thorns. Thorns supplied, not by the foster-father or the foster-mother, but by the boys, who, once they had extracted full particulars of Bobbie's adventure, made from these facts ammunition for gay badinage that, well aimed, gave them great content. In school, the game was played furtively. A slip of paper would be passed along the forms of the fourth standard class bearing the inquiry of a seeker after knowledge, "Who pinched the cornet?" this would be varied by rough sketches executed by Master Nutler of a lad running, with the words underneath, "Hold him!" When Bobbie strolled out of school at dinner time there would come an affected cry of alarm, "He's off again!" Robert Lancaster took all of this with stolidity and in a manner differing from that which he would have exhibited a month previously. It seemed that the failure of his expedition had tamed him; certainly his stay in the hospital and at the convalescent home had given him reticence. He applied himself to his lessons. After a few weeks the other boys declined to be led any longer by Master Nutler, because there seemed little sport in rallying a man who showed no signs of annoyance, and Bobbie Lancaster presently found—excepting for an occasional reminder—that the Brenchley escapade had gone out of memory. Miss Nutler on one of the rare occasions when they met, expressed her regret at the consequences of their disagreement, hinting that, so far as she was concerned, the past could be shut out from memory.

"It was my eldest brother put me up to it," said Miss Nutler apologetically. "You know what a one he is."

"I do," remarked Master Lancaster.

"I should never 'ave thought of it if it hadn't been for him," declared Miss Nutler. "A better hearted girl than me you wouldn't find in a day's march."

"Dessay!"

"In fact," went on the young person, waxing enthusiastic, "I'm too good-hearted for this world. I'm a fool to meself. And that's why I gave way when he told me to pretend you'd hurt me. See?"

"I see."

"And so long as you say there's no ill-will and so long as you agree to forgive and forget, so to speak, why there's no reason, as you remarked just now, why we shouldn't be capital friends."

"I never said no such thing," said the boy.

"Didn't you?" said Miss Nutler wonderingly. "Words to that effect, then."

"No! Not words to that effect, neither."

"You're back in the band, aren't you?"

"I am back in the band."

"All the girls in our cottage rave about your cornet playing."

"Straight?" He could not help smiling at this generous compliment.

"As if I should tell a lie," said Miss Nutler. "Why, they're always talking about you. How you've growed and how you've improved in your manner and—there! I tell you. I get quite jealous sometimes."

"What call have you to be jealous?"

"Oh, dear! oh, dear!" said the young woman self-reproachfully. "Now I've been and let the cat out of the bag. That's me all the world over. I never meant you to see that I was—hem—fond of you."

"Put all ideas of that out of your red young crumpet," he advised steadily, "as soon as ever you like."

"Is there somebody else?" asked Miss Nutler, flushing.

"Since you ask the question—yes."

"Does she live 'ere at the Homes?"

"She does not live 'ere at the Homes."

"If she did," said Miss Nutler fiercely, "I'd pay her out, the cat. And you're a double-faced boy, you are. I wouldn't be seen talking to you for fifty thousand pounds."

"I guessed that was the amount."

Miss Nutler walked off aflame with annoyance, turning as she reached the gate and making a face not pretty, in order that Bobbie might understand the true state of her feelings. That evening one of the Nutler family handed Bobbie a note on which was written, "Dear sir, referring to our meeting, I beg to inform you that all is over between us. Yours obed'tly, Louisa Nutler.—P.S. A reply by bearer will oblige." Bobbie tore the note into many pieces, threw them over the messenger, and going indoors penned a careful note to Mrs. Bell, of Pimlico Walk. This contained an account of his progress; contained also five words, "Give my love to Trixie," which note, reaching the Walk the next morning, made so much sunshine for the industrious young lady that she proceeded to scrub the stairs from top to basement in order to prevent herself from becoming light-headed.

There was indeed progress to report. The Fourth Standard being carried by assault, his brain had now to wrestle in the large schoolroom with dogged enemies of youth.

By the help of an assistant master, whose stock of enthusiasm had not been quite exhausted by lads of the Nutler brand, Bobbie showed excellent fight, and if it sometimes happened that he was worsted, the defeats were but temporary. Winter came, and with it football matches. An eminent three-quarter (who was also a trombone) having retired from the team during the off season in order to take up duties at Kneller Hall, Bobbie, in games with private schools, found himself selected for the position. The drill-sergeant took interest in the lad, and on the boarded-over swimming-bath, instructed him carefully at five o'clock each evening in the art of vaulting. All this helped to make a solid youth of Robert Lancaster, and he found himself wishful for manhood.

The Sister at the infirmary beyond the western gates, having to take a month's holiday, a friend of hers came to act as substitute, and this friend proving to be Sister Margaret, Bobbie found an additional incentive for correct behaviour because Sister Margaret, when going down at any time the broad gravelled road between the cottages, always selected him for one of her cheerful bows, causing Bobbie's cap to fly off in acknowledgment and making him flush with gratification. Sister Margaret told him that Myddleton West had gone to Ireland for one of the daily journals, and together they read his letters in that journal. It seemed clear that Sister Margaret continued to have no objection to talking about Myddleton West, for she made the boy describe several times over the morning when he had called at his rooms in Fetter Lane; at each repetition Bobbie managed to find (or to invent) some additional incident that made the young woman's bright eyes become brighter with interest. When the regular Sister returned, Sister Margaret had to leave, and Bobbie walked with her to the station to carry her portmanteau, giving much good advice on the way with view of doing a good turn for his friend. Apparently his arguments made some impression on Sister Margaret, for when, as the train went off, he shouted, "Give my kind respects to him, Miss, when you write. And tell him he ain't forgotten," it looked as though the young woman's bright eyes became suddenly wet.

The seasons passed. The fourteenth birthday came so near that it was quite possible to reckon the interval by number of days. For some months Robert Lancaster had been a half-timer; he desired now to say good-bye definitely to school, and to go into the workshops, because this would be a conspicuous milestone marking his journey. The Coastguard and the Coastguard's daughter, and the long Customs' officer came to see him on one of the later days, and he showed them with pride the tailor's shop, the bootmaker's shop, the carpenter's shop, and the engineer's shop, and Coastguard and himself (whilst the tall daughter went with the representative of her Majesty's Customs to take tea at the hotel opposite the gates) talked over questions of trades, and their various advantages. They weighed them separately; when the young couple returned, Coastguard with a look of wisdom that judges of Appeal try to assume and cannot, delivered his decision. Bobbie, interested in this, saw the long Customs' officer snatch a kiss from Coastguard's daughter with no feeling of jealousy, and, indeed, with diversion.

"Nothing like helping yourself," remarked Bobbie, amused.

"Do give over, John," said Coastguard's daughter reprovingly. "You never know when to stop."

"These youngsters," said Bobbie to Coastguard paternally, "they will carry on, won't they? Same now as it was in our young day."

"Dang the boy's eyes," said Coastguard, "if he don't notice everything."

"It makes anyone," said Bobbie, "when you see a couple young enough to know better a kissin' each other."

"You're supposed not to notice such things at your age," said the angel reprovingly.

"Ah," said the boy, acutely, "supposed not."

"Reckon you'll be the next one we shall hear of getting engaged."

"Many a true word spoke in jest," said the boy. "And you think," turning with seriousness to the Coastguard, "you think I can't do better than go in for learning that?"

"Sure of it, my boy."

Therefore to the engineer's shop went Bobbie, because the Coastguard had pointed out to him that some of the knowledge to be gained there could not fail some day to be valuable. Not that he intended to become an engineer. Decision as to his first occupation on leaving the Home had already been taken, being preserved as a secret which he proposed not to disclose until the appropriate moment came. At the tables in the engineer's shop he worked, and learned under direction, after some failures, how to use a lathe without pinching his fingers. The lads worked in extra garments of aprons and paper caps; their task made them so grimy that they felt sure no one could tell them from adults; the wash that came after a day in the workshop seemed to put them back ten years. An increased feeling of maturity came to Bobbie when, on being selected to play "The Lost Chord," as a cornet solo at a concert in the neighbourhood which the Home's band attended, a local paper called him by a fascinating misprint Mister Robert Lancaster, intending to say Master, but allowing the i's to have it. He walked rigidly upright for several weeks after this and spoke to no boy under the age of thirteen.

"You fancy yourself," remarked sarcastically the boys whom he ignored.

"I do," he replied, frankly.

It became his keen endeavour at this period to reach at least four feet six in height. He had special reasons for this ambition, and days occurred when, in his impatience, he measured himself three times during the twenty-four hours. The last inch seemed as though it would never arrive; other lads in the engineer's shop, to encourage him, expressed the cheerful opinion that he had stopped growing. Finding in a newspaper an advertisement specially addressed "To the Short," he wrote privately to Trixie Bell to obtain for him the golden remedy that the advertisers promised to send on receipt of two shillings and ninepence, and when Trixie, glad of an opportunity for being useful, obeyed, sending him the result as a birthday present, "With kind regards," Bobbie found that the remedy was but a pair of thick list soles to be worn inside the boots; he perceived hopelessly that nothing could be done to encourage Nature. The last pencil mark on the wall of his dormitory denoting his height remained as a record for months; depression enveloped him when he gazed at it. But there came a spring season when he found to his intense delight that he had, within a brief period, not only shot up to the necessary inches, but just beyond them, and the mother of Collingwood Cottage had to lengthen the arms of his jackets and the legs of his trousers. On being measured anew in the tailor's shop, he laughed with sheer delight.

The day of all days came.

"Father wants to see you, Lancaster," announced one of the other lads.

"What's up?"

"Committee day," said the other lad.

Robert Lancaster ran off to find the Collingwood father, and came up to him breathless. The Collingwood father was a serious man, made more serious by his family of other people's children; his face took now an aspect of importance, and he laid his hand on the lad's shoulder.

"Time's come," he said.

"Three cheers," said Bobbie.

"Keep cool, my lad."

"I am cool," said Bobbie, trembling with eagerness.

"Don't forget that the gentlemen, what you are going now to have an interview with, represent so to speak your benefactors what have looked after you and clothed you and fed you and generally speaking kept you flourishing."

"I know what you mean."

"You'll go before the Committee," said the father of Collingwood Cottage, solemnly, "and what I want to impress upon you, my boy, is the necessity of putting on your very best manners. A little bad behaviour on your part will go a long way."

"I'll watch out, father."

"You can't be too civil," urged the father of Collingwood, anxiously. "I tell you that, Bobbie, because, naturally, you ain't what I call the humblest chap going, and if you want these nobs to agree to what you want, you must show 'em any amount of what I may venture to call deference."

"I'll lick all the bloomin' blackin' off their bloomin' boots," promised Bobbie.

"Give your 'ands another wash," recommended the father, "and then go up."

The Superintendent stood at the side of the table; seated there were half-a-dozen men who looked like, and indeed were, retired tradesmen. In one of them the lad recognized the carpenter (now in white waistcoat and with other signs of prosperity) who had been on the jury which had investigated, years ago, the death of his mother. A cheery red-faced man sat in the large arm-chair.

"Robert Lancaster, gentlemen, fourteen years of age and a good lad with a fairly good record, has passed the Fourth Standard, and is one of the best of our bandsmen."

"Now, my lad!" The jovial-looking chairman pointed the ruler at him. "What would you like to be? We've fed you and educated you and brought you up, and we don't want to see all the trouble wasted."

"Moreover," said the carpenter, as Bobbie prepared to speak, "it's a question on which, by rights, you ought to take our advice. We're men of the world, and as such we know what's good for you a jolly sight better than you do. My argument has always been that pauper children—"

The chairman coughed.

"Or whatever you like to call 'em ought not to be allowed to pick and choose. It pampers 'em," said the carpenter, gloomily, sending his penholder, nib downwards, into the table, "I don't care what you say; it pampers 'em."

"I should like, sir, please," said Bobbie, "to—"

"Choose a honest trade," suggested the carpenter.

"Let the boy speak," urged one of the other members.

"I should like to be a sailor," said the lad.

"Ah!" said the carpenter, triumphantly. "What did I tell you?"

"Our band boys don't often go into the navy," said the Superintendent. "Most of them go in for the other branch of the service."

"Jolly good thing," said the gloomy carpenter, with his fingers in the pockets of his white waistcoat, "if all your armies and all your navies was done away with and abolished."

"Talk sense!" advised his neighbour.

"What are they," asked the carpenter, "but a tax on the respectable tradesmen of this country? What good are they? What do they do? That's what I want to know." He looked round at his colleagues with the confident air of one propounding a riddle of which none knew the answer. "Will someone kindly tell me what good the navy does? What benefit does it do me or any of us seated at this table? If all our ships was to disappear this very morning before twelve o'clock struck, should I be any the worse off?"

"Why, you silly old silly," broke in the lad on the other side of the table, impetuously, "if that was to 'appen some foreign power would be down on us before you could wink, and you'd find yourself—"

"Silence!" ordered the Superintendent.

"Find yourself," persisted Bobbie, "turned into a bloomin' Russian very like, and sent to Siberia."

"You have your answer," remarked the chairman, jovially.

"Kids' talk," growled the carpenter.

"Why," declared Bobbie, "it's the only protection you've got to enable you to carry on your business peaceably and successfully, and without interference."

"I never felt the want of no navy in carryin' on my business in Shoreditch."

"Course you didn't," said Bobbie. "But if there hadn't been a navy you would."

It was all very irregular; the Superintendent felt this, but the members of the committee showed so much gratification in seeing their colleague routed that it scarce seemed right for him to interfere. The chairman rapped gently on the table as a mild reminder that order appeared to be temporarily absent.

"Fact of it is," said the carpenter, resentfully, "you youngsters get so pampered—"

"Come, come!" said the chairman, "let us get along. You think you'll like the navy, my lad?"

"Sure of it, sir."

"It's a hard life, mind you. Especially at first."

"Shan't mind that, sir."

"You'll undergo pretty severe preparation; we shall have to find out from the doctor whether you can stand it or not. Her Majesty doesn't want half and half sort of lads in her navy."

"I think I shall be all right, sir. I've improved wonderful in the years I've been here."

"Made a man of you, have we?"

"You have that, sir," said Bobbie.

"Well, then—"

"Something was said," interrupted the carpenter, still smarting, "about this lad having a fairly good record. I should like to be kindly informed what his record actually is. If there's anything against him it's only right and fair and honest and just that we should know about it now."

The Superintendent explained, and Robert Lancaster went white at the lips as he heard the account—by no means a harsh account—of his escape from the Homes.

"Since which time," added the Superintendent, "his conduct has been most exemplary."

"Thank you, sir," burst out the lad.

"And this is the lad," argued the carpenter, "that you're going to spend more of the ratepayers' money on. This is the lad that's cost us a matter of thirty pound a year for the last four years, and now we're going to send him off to a training ship, where he'll cost us a matter of thirty-two pound a year. Is that so, or is it not so?"

"It is so," said the chairman.

"It's enough," declared the retired carpenter, gloomily, "to make a man give up public life altogether. What was he when we begun to have to do with him? Answer me, somebody."

The Superintendent asked if the information was really necessary.

"Pardon me, sir," said Robert Lancaster, from the other side of the table. "I can give the information what's required. I was left without parents, I was, and I become the 'sociate of bad characters. My coming down 'ere put me on the straight, and I tell you I ain't particular anxious to get off of it."

"My lad!" said the jovial chairman, "we'll see that you don't. You'll have a couple of years on the training ship, and when you leave there I hope you'll make up your mind to be a credit to your parish, to your country, and your Queen."

"Hooray!" said Robert Lancaster, softly.

"And we shall look to you to see that all this money which has been spent on you is not wasted. We shall expect you to become a good citizen, one who will help in some small way to improve the estimate in which his great country is held."

"Bah!" said the carpenter. But the other members of the committee said, "Hear, hear."

"Come back and see the Homes when you get an opportunity," said the jovial chairman, a little moved by his own eloquence; "remember that we shall watch your career with interest and—God bless you!"

The chairman leaned across the table and shook hands with Robert. The lad bowed awkwardly to the other members of the committee, and would have spoken, but something in his throat prevented him. He punched at his cap, and on a signal from the Superintendent went out at the doorway.

"Pampering of 'em," said the retired carpenter, darkly, "pampering of 'em as fast as ever you can."


CHAPTER XIV

The vessel to which Bobbie went had been in its gallant youth a battleship and possessed an eventful and a creditable record. Moored in the Thames off the flat coast of Essex, and painted black, it was a huge, solid, responsible three-decker, doing excellent work in the autumn of its life, and giving temporary residence to some five or six hundred boys. Mainly, the youngsters were metropolitan, but sometimes the guardians of distant towns in the North would arrange with the Board for one of their lads to be consigned to the training ship, who, being arrived, spoke a language that seemed to the London boys almost foreign. A long, low jetty ran from the shore as far as it dared into the water; where it stopped, a gig rowed by eight of the boys, under the command of an officer, took you off to the big black ship, on the starboard side of which a dozen small boats rocked and nudged each other in the ribs, and a barge dozed stolidly. (In case of alarm the whole of the boys could be cleared out of the ship and carried away by these to safety.) Away down the river a smart brigantine berthed generally in view, and this the boys who intended to join the Royal Navy gazed at hopefully, because it was the brigantine which taught them seamanship, with assistance from a master mariner and two mates; it was the brigantine, too, which now and again skimmed the cream of the Westmouth in the shape of some forty boys whom it conveyed out of the river into the open, and presently down Channel to one of the training vessels which acted as the last refining process before entrance was made into the service. To the Essex shore came, nearly every week, from various poor-law schools, boys who, after inspection, were conveyed out to the Westmouth, where the captain looked at the doctor's report, giving their heights, chest measurements, and other particulars forming the foundation of their dossier. This over, the new boys went back to shore to be clothed in sailor uniform, and re-appeared in blue serge trousers and jacket and cap, trying to look as though the navy had for them no secrets, and the Westmouth nothing in the way of information to impart. They came in and went out of the training vessel at the rate of about three hundred year, so that the numbered white cases down on the lower deck containing kits were always in use, and every hammock on the three decks contained at night a tired-out lad.

For Robert Lancaster soon discovered that the note of the Westmouth was to keep moving. If you worked, you worked hard; if you played, you played hard. School had no great demands upon him now, for being out of the Fourth Standard, it was required of him that he should attend but two hours on the Friday of every week; a boy might have assumed that with this dispensation one could look forward to a life of ease and content. Not so on board the Westmouth. Robert Lancaster was never allowed to be lazy. The life formed an exact opposite to those old days at Hoxton (several centuries ago it seemed to him), when the delight of life was to "mouch," which, translated, is to wander through the years aimlessly. Robert made some vague suggestions of reform to his comrades, with the result that a boy from Poplar made up his mind to state a complaint formally on the first opportunity. The Poplar boy (numbered 290) had already written a brief account, which he had shown to Robert, entitled "The Mutiny on the Westmouth," a forecast of a somewhat bloodthirsty character, where gore flowed readily, and exclamations of a melodramatic character were used, such as "Die, you dog!" and "At last we meet face to face!" but Robert criticized this with some acidity, because in the course of it Number Two Ninety himself performed all the deeds of surpassing valour, using six Martini-Henry rifles and a field gun, at the same time doing desperate action with two cutlasses: the end of the account gave a gruesome description of the upper deck strewn with the bodies of officers, and of Number Two Ninety-being unanimously elected captain by his fellow mutineers. Robert said he thought the picture overdrawn. Opportunity, however, occurred on some of the guardians from Poplar visiting the ship; one, a sharp clergyman, demanded to know of the Poplar boys whether they had any complaint to make.

"No, sir," sang most of the Poplar boys. The mutineer's arm went up.

"Ah!" said the clergyman gratified. "Here's a lad now who has something to say."

"Step forward, Two Ninety," ordered the old captain. "Tell this gentleman what it is you wish to complain of. Is it the food?"

"Grub's all right, sir," growled the Poplar boy.

"Is it the uniform?" asked the sharp clergyman.

"No fault to find with the clothes, sir."

"Is it the ship?"

"Ship's good enough, sir."

Robert Lancaster, passing with a pail, half stopped to hear what the Poplar boy would say under this process of exhaustion.

"Well, well, what is the complaint you wish to make?"

Two Ninety from Poplar twisted his sailor's cap nervously, and looked with some interest at his shoes.

"Well, sir," he burst out, "it's like this. They always keep on making you keep on."

Robert Lancaster, finding after a few weeks that his disinclination to continuous work and exercise had vanished, detached himself therefore from the small set on the Westmouth, called "The Born-Tireds." After the fifth week privileges came to him; he was allowed to go ashore with the other boys on Sunday afternoon; he joined in the drill, and this he liked so much that he concealed from the officers the fact that the cornet and he were close acquaintances, fearing that membership of the band, which practised far away down in the hold, would interfere. He found books in the library with a sea flavour, and read Stevenson and Henty, and Clark Russell. He liked Clark Russell's books, because they had always one admirable young lady in a distressful predicament, and this young lady he always thought of as being Trixie Bell—Trixie who had sent him her photograph, taken by an eminent artist of Hackney Road, and presenting her as in a snowstorm, with no hat, a basket of choice roses on her arm. At prayers one night, Robert found himself, somewhat to his surprise, introducing a special silent reference to Trixie, and, pleased with his daring originality, he continued it, feeling in a shy, half-ashamed way, that he had now assumed a responsible position in regard to the young lady. For the rest, there was not much time on the Westmouth to think of outside affairs.

He found his average day made up in this manner. At six o'clock in the morning, the lower deck, where he and some three hundred other boys slept, became suddenly filled with the blaring of a bugle; on the instant Robert slipped out of his hammock. The chief petty officers (important lads of about fifteen or sixteen) issued orders, the boys dressed swiftly, hammocks were rolled up and stowed away at the sides, and then the busy working day began. Robert Lancaster, despatched with other gallant sailors of his division, scrubbed the upper deck (protected by a canvas awning in summer, and an awning and curtains in winter), the while two divisions saw to the main deck. Then the upper deck had to be swabbed, under the superintendence of the ship's officers, and, this done, breakfast-time had arrived. Robert Lancaster always felt the better for his breakfast, being, indeed, of the growing age when appetite is nearly ever acute and demanding to be satisfied. The watch on the mess deck cleared away, and at half-past eight one bell sounded. At nine o'clock two bells sounded, with the singers' call for prayers and also for punishments, at which hour a few boys with correction looming close to them, wished that they had chosen the life of a landsman. The excellent old captain's theory was that you should either pat a boy on the back or cane him on the back, and this system worked out very well in practice; the most severe punishment consisted of a few hours' solitude in the dark cell at the foc'sle end of the ship—an extreme remedy resorted to but once or twice a year. Prayers and punishment being over, there occurred work again. Sail-making, painting the sides of the Westmouth, seamanship instruction; in the tailors' shop, manufacture of flags, repairing of oilskins and sou'westers, lengthening of trousers for their growing owners, making of seamanship stripes, re-covering of life-belts; the biggest boys in the Rigger's class called upon to strip and serve afresh the lower rigging of the ship. Relaxation came to Robert when sent out with others in one of the small boats which clustered at the side of the Westmouth, on which occasions he learnt the arts of boat-pulling and boat-sailing, under the guidance of a giant-voiced officer, who roared advice and frank criticism. Signalling had to be learnt, and this demanded of Robert that his intelligence should be livened; the lad being on his mettle, and having made up his mind to extort the secrets from this cryptic procedure, earned commendation. There were classes in gunnery, too, where knowledge was gained in using the rifle and cutlass, as well as the management of field guns; the rifles full-sized, and, indeed, a little out of proportion to the height of the smaller boys, so that it sometimes seemed that it would have been easier for the Martini-Henry to manage the boy than for the boy to manage the Martini-Henry. And about mid-day, after half an hour's rest, when Robert bowled boys out on the upper deck, or being at the wickets set in a wooden socket, sent the ball flying away to the Essex shore, came dinner. Now dinner on the Westmouth, mind you, was dinner.

A bugle call brought the boys scurrying down the broad hatchway on to the mess deck, where a harmonium had been placed in position, and, as they hurried down, adjusting their red handkerchiefs bib-fashion, the cook's assistants dragged young lorries around by the long wooden tables, one waggon loaded with roast beef, another waggon carrying potatoes, another bearing vegetables and another bread. The boys on sharp days when appetite had become keen found it difficult to sing the grace to which the harmonium played a prelude, because their mouths watered. The scent from the roast beef was to them the most entrancing perfume, and ranged in companies they could not prevent their eyes from wandering to their table where portions were being served out in the deep tin plates. A bugle call—everything on board the Westmouth was done by bugle calls; and none was so effective as the call for silence—and grace.

"Be present at our table, Lord,
Be 'ere and everywhere adored;
These creatures bless, and grant that we
May feast in Paradise with Thee."

On ordinary days, work re-commenced in the afternoon with occasional brief rests for play, and after tea if there still remained work to do it had to be done. Strict orders had to be observed in the way of behaviour, and Robert slipped into these with greater ease because of his experience in the Cottage Homes. He learnt that an order being given, obedience had to follow instantly and without question; the saluting of the officers was, he knew, but a respectful sign of his willingness to comply with this rule. In this way Robert Lancaster learnt discipline.

"It's easy enough," argued Robert to the Poplar boy when he had been on the ship for nearly a year and was looking forward to the position of Chief Petty Officer with three stripes on his arm and a salary of penny a week, "once you get into the swing of it. If you do have to put up with a bit of rough, you've always got your Wednesdays to look forward to."

Wednesday, indeed, represented the golden day of the week for the Westmouth. Friends came then on permission of the Captain, and when one evening a letter from Trixie Bell was brought over to the ship by the post boy, a letter which asked her dear Robert to obtain a permit for two, the lad procured this and sent it off with bashful anticipation of seeing the young lady and her large mother. The afternoon came, and he watched each arrival of the gig from the shore for the first sight of Trixie; wondering amusedly how Mrs. Bell would endure the brief passage and how she would be hauled out of the boat. But Trixie did not arrive nor did her mother come to endanger the safety of the gig; instead Number Three Thirty-Three (who was Robert) found himself called to receive a mite of a woman in a sailor hat bearing the inscription H.M.S. Magnificent in large gold letters, who having come up the ladder at the side of the ship one step at a time, now stood with a net full of oranges and cakes beside her; her hands at her waist as though doubtful whether she ought not to dance a hornpipe, and looking up at Robert with her bead-like eyes full of astonishment.

"Why," cried little Miss Threepenny, "if he hasn't grown up to be a reg'lar what's a name."

"I was expecting two others," remarked Robert, bending shyly to shake hands.

"They couldn't come and they sent me instead," said the little woman, mopping her forehead with her handkerchief. "Poor Mrs. Bell is as bad as bad, and Trixie—bless her 'eart—wouldn't think of leaving her. So I says, 'Sposin' I go?' And Trixie says, 'You, Miss Threepenny?' and I says, 'Yes, me. It's my annual 'oliday from Tabernacle Street Wednesday next, and—'"

"And here you are."

"'Why,' says Trixie," went on the small woman, declining to anticipate the end of her story, "'you'll go and get lost.' And I says, 'Stuff and nonsense; if a grown-up woman of forty can't take care of herself, who can? Besides,' I says, 'I want to see the dear boy.' And Trixie says, 'So did I.'"

"Oh, she said that, did she?" remarked Robert gratified. Other boys crowded round, preparing to invent humorous badinage.

"Ah!" said Miss Threepenny acutely, "and what's more, she meant it."

It required some courage for a boy of Robert's age to escort the amazing little woman over the ship; urgent whispers from the other lads to be introduced to the new missis did not assist him. The Chief Officer nodded approvingly, and this gave encouragement.

"Booking clerk at Fenchurch Street," chattered on the little woman, "gave me 'alf a ticket, and I gave him a bit of my mind. People think because I ain't so tall as I might be that I 'aren't got a tongue in me 'ead. They find out their mistake."

"Is Mrs. Bell very ill?"

"She ain't much longer for this world," answered Miss Threepenny. "She may linger on for a year or two, but that good young gel of hers will be left all alone in the world before she's very much older. Fortunately she's got a wise 'ead on young shoulders and—What low ceilings they are 'ere." The little woman bent her small body from an entirely unfounded fear of touching the roof with her sailor hat. "What's this part of the ship called, Bobbie?"

"This," explained the lad, "is called the foc'sle."

"Why?"

"Ah!" said Robert, "'why' is the one word you mustn't use on board ship."

Little Miss Threepenny trotted round, breathless with the endeavour to keep up with the lad's stride, presently thanking her stars in earnest terms when, the hour being two, she was allowed to sit on the foc'sle steps of the upper deck in company with a few mothers and sisters to watch the afternoon's entertainment.

"I shall 'ave to take notice of everything," she chirruped, "and go through it all when I get back to Pimlico Walk. Trixie will want to 'ear about it."

"Don't you go and get frightened," urged Robert.

"Me frightened?"

"There'll be some desperate deeds performed during the next hour," said Robert importantly.

"So long as there's no firing of guns," said the little woman, adjusting her skirts precisely, "I shan't so much as wink. Once they begin to bang away—"

Two of the women visitors who had been looking curiously at the small creature, hastened to remark with the knowledge born of experience that there would be firing, one adding that for her part she always shut her eyes and put her hands over her ears when it came to that part; an ingenious plan which happy Miss Threepenny promised to adopt. Robert ran off and disappeared.

The alarming clang, clang, clang of a bell! Upon the instant, a swift rushing to and fro; a throwing open of the door leading to the captain's room; boys with buckets of water hurrying up and forming in line; more boys dragging long boa constrictors of leathern hose up to the doorway; still more boys ready with brass nozzles to fix on; more boys again in a tremendous state of excitement bearing scarlet extincteurs on their backs; a white-capped, white-aproned cook up from below and assisting; sharp commands from the officers; the old captain watching all with his watch open. "Good," says the captain of the Westmouth presently, "very good indeed. Who was the first bucket up, Mr. Waltham?" "Number Three Fifty-Two, sir," says the chief officer. "Three Fifty-Two," thereupon says the captain, "catch this sixpence."

Band now at a corner of the upper deck, with a stout drum placed upon trestles, to be whacked presently as though it had committed some gross breach of discipline. Music-stands up; brass instruments tested; the bandmaster taps his wooden stand sharply. Three hundred boys in detachments on either side of the deck; first officer, with a voice accustomed to open-air speaking, with the captain on the poop. A brief drill, and then,—

"Form divisions!"

"Right about face!"

"March!"

The band plays; the two broad, close, moving detachments go steadily around. A roar from the chief officer, and at once the broad masses become a number of thin strands with a serpentine movement to a new and more cheerful march from the band, and doing it with absolute accuracy for several minutes. "Halt!" Music stops.

"Boys," shouts the old captain from the poop, "very fair, very fair indeed! Eh, Mr. Waltham?"

"Very fair indeed, sir."

A selection made from the crowd; the rest jump up on the sides of the ship, and become an audience. The selected boys stiffly in line, jackets off, accept from a chief petty officer with a sack, pairs of wooden dumb-bells. Order given, they face round, watching the instructor narrowly and with seriousness. A signal from him and band having started a gentle waltz, the two hundred sailor boys go through a movement of thrusting the arms forward, withdrawing them sharply, keeping time ever to the music. A change of air on the part of the band, and each pair of arms swings from side to side. Another, and with clockwork preciseness the bells are up high, return to touch breast, go down to toes. A whole dozen of these changes, and amongst the later ones, movements with definite stamp of the right foot on the deck to the music of a Scotch reel. Pantomime rally from the band; a bugle call, and the deck is clear.

"If I hadn't seen it," says astounded little Miss Threepenny to her two neighbours, and standing now on the topmost stair of the foc'sle steps, "I should never 'ave believed it true!"

"That's nothing," remarks one of the women, lightly. "You watch out now, Miss. My Jimmy's in the next."

To a march from the obliging band, enter forty serious boys, brown-legginged, belted, and bearing rifles. At the words of command, these go through a number of offensive and defensive movements, forming squares, performing cutlass drill, making lunges with their bayonetted rifles at a supposititious enemy; killing this supposititious enemy and withdrawing the bayonet neatly from his lifeless body. A good quarter of an hour of hard drill this, for which they are more than repaid by applause from the younger boys seated on the sides of the vessel, and a word of approval from the captain:

"'Ere comes Bobbie," cries Miss Threepenny, excitedly. "Oh, dear! oh, dear! what will they be up to next?"

Mothers seated on the steps may well start and clutch each other's arms, for field guns are being dragged on now by straw-hatted detachments, and, to a brisk air from the band, tugged by long ropes around and around the deck.

"There he is," cries Miss Threepenny, excitedly. "There he is again. And there he is once more."

No time for Robert to take notice of the little woman's shrill comments, even if the bustle allowed him to hear, for field guns are things that demand attention jealously. An order pulls them up short; Robert with eight other lads stopping their gun on the starboard side. Every boy panting; every boy with his flushed face directed towards the chief officer on the poop. A shrill whistle.

"Dismount!" shouts the chief officer.

Fierce attack on the guns, wheels off, axles unpinned, guns lifted, remainder of carriage pulled to pieces, all down flat on the deck, boy seated on them and looking up at the poop for comment.

"Fifteen seconds, Mr. Waltham."

"Fifteen, sir," says the chief officer respectfully; "fifteen as near as a toucher."

"They did it in less time last week, Mr. Waltham."

"They did it in less time last week, sir," replies the chief officer.

The old captain shakes his head first at the scarlet-faced lads seated on the portions of their gun carriages and then at his watch, as though inclined to blame the watch as much as the boys. The instructor goes from one set of lads to another growling a word of advice.

"Re-mount!"

Every boy to his feet; the parts of the carriage seized; wheels held in place and fixed; the heavy gun lifted and slung, carriage pushed forward to catch it in position. Robert's detachment, to their great annoyance and confusion, find all their quick efforts retarded by the clumsiness of Number Eight, who, having mistaken his duties, has come into collision with another boy, and seems inclined to argue the matter out and prove himself thoroughly in the wrong before anything further is done. At least six seconds lost by this action on the part of Number Eight in Robert Lancaster's gun, so that the other five guns are all perfect and their boys standing cool and serene, whilst the final struggle is being concluded on the starboard side.

"I rather want that movement concluded to-day," says the old captain, leaning over and speaking ironically.

"What's your number?" asks the instructor of the offending boy.

"Eight, sir."

"Ah," remarks the instructor, "it might as well be nought. Isn't your place there? Very well, then."

"Try that again, boys," cries the chief officer. "Do it sharper this time. Think what you're about."

Thought and celerity and earnestness are all brought to bear on the next dismounting, and Number Eight of Robert's set, reserving justification for his previous conduct, proves himself as able a seaman as the rest. The remounting is performed with similar swiftness, and the old captain lets the case of his watch close with a snap and says, leaning over the rails again and addressing the boys on deck, "Very good, very good indeed. Eh, Mr. Waltham?" "Very good indeed, sir," agrees the chief officer.

Fierce business coming now! The white-headed mops go down the nozzles of the guns, come out again, the gunners stand clear, one lad jerks a string, and—bang! White mop down again head first and withdrawn, gun sighted, and again—bang! It being unusual for an attacking force to do this dangerous work without casualty, half a dozen boys affect to receive the fire of the unseen enemy and fall on deck screaming with great anguish, "Oh, oh, oh!" and "'Elp, 'elp, 'elp!" to the great consternation of one mother up near the foc'sle, who is with difficulty restrained from rushing down the steps. Ambulance corps hurries forward; one wounded boy has his trousers pulled up, his bared leg set between two pieces of wood and tied up, a stretcher brought, and he is taken, now giving agonizing groans, which have a fine suggestion of pathos, to the port side deck. Other boys who have fallen victims to the non-existent enemy have their arms placed in slings or their heads bandaged, and are led away by sympathetic ambulance men.

"Sound for the march past, bugler."

Band, which has been interested in this scene of carnage, snatches up its instruments and starts a cheerful, brisk, trotting air; the boys take the ropes and tug the guns on the field carriages once around the deck, the wounded following in the rear and still giving realistic groans at every other step, all disappearing at last through the large doors of the foc'sle to the applause of boys seated on the sides and fluttering of handkerchiefs from the foc'sle steps.

"Bray'vo, Bobbie," cries little Miss Threepenny. She turns and whispers apprehensively to the two women. "They're none of 'em reelly 'urt, are they?"

"'Urt?" echoes one of the two women. "They know better than go and get 'urt, bless you."

"All the same," says the little woman, "I wouldn't join in it for forty thousand million pound."

The rifle lads again, faces set determinedly, marching up the deck with steady and definite stride. Four movements, and they are down on one knee preparing to receive the enemy. This time the enemy is no fictitious enemy, for the doors of the foc'sle being thrown open, out rush shrieking noisy warriors who from their language and the fact that they are carrying long poles instead of firearms are clearly negro aborigines of the district, and these shout "Alla-bulla-wulla" in a very desperate way, throwing themselves on their opponents under the foolish impression that something can be done to a solid square of British sailors. A bugle call and the square rises, moves, and taking the offensive, presses the mistaken aborigines back, but these still cry "Alla-bulla-walla" (being apparently of a race with limited conversational powers), and break up the detachment, so that a hand-to-hand struggle ensues where every man carries his life in peril, and every man remembers the country that gave him birth. The British are pulled together again; they form by command into two lines, these two lines stretching well across the field of operations press the enemy slowly but determinedly back. Changing its tactics the enemy now shout, "Wulla-bulla-alla," but even this reversal of the original battle cry proves useless, and the final struggle is stopped (because in point of fact, one or two sets are beginning to fight in real earnest) by the bugle call to retreat. Victory gained, the British sailors re-form, and singing exultant music to—

"A life on the ocean wave,
A life on the stormy deep,
Where the billowy waters wave,
And the stars their vigil keep,"

they march round and pass the saluting point.

"Not at all bad," says the captain. "Eh, Mr. Waltham? Considering."

"Not at all bad, sir," replies the chief officer, "considering."

Robert escorted his little visitor down to tea, a few of his intimate chums forming a circle around her in order to prevent the incursion of mere curiosity. Miss Threepenny, finding herself the object and centre of all this consideration, chattered away over her tea and bread and butter, telling the circle a few of her best repartees, with many a "Oh, I says," and "What! she says"; each recital finishing triumphantly with the sentence, "And that's all they get for trying to score off me." The small woman being swung down to the lower deck, professed herself much shocked at seeing the slung-up hammocks, declaring that eviction from her model dwellings would ensue if this were known, and covering her face with her tiny hands in a way that amused the lads very much. Before leaving she ascertained the whereabouts of Robert's locker, and finding the white box with Robert's number painted atop, slipped inside an envelope containing a silver coin of enormous proportions. On the upper deck again, Robert Lancaster feeling it politic to do everything possible in order to give Miss Threepenny subject-matter for conversation on her return to Trixie, went up to the foc'sle rigging to the foretop and was down again before she had time to beg of him to be careful, following this up by acts of a similarly perilous nature.

"How in the world I shall find breath enough to tell 'em all about you," she said distractedly, "goodness only knows."

"Don't forget to mention," said Robert, "that I'm going to be made a chief petty officer next week."

"And how long did you say it'd be before you left?"

"I shan't stay long," he said importantly. "They want chaps in the Royal Navy, and I'm five foot one already."

"They 'ave made a man of you, Bobbie," declared the little woman, looking up at him admiringly. "Nobody'd think to look at you now that it was only a few years ago you was nothing more or less than—"

"Just put your 'and on my arm," interrupted Robert rather hastily. "Above the elbow, I mean. Now then!" He drew his arm up slowly, and the muscles stood out hard and rigid.

"You're nothing more nor less," said Miss Threepenny, "than what they call in books a Herkools. And— and you've quite made up your mind to be a sailor, Bobbie."

"Of Her Majesty's Navy," said Bobbie proudly. "There's the signal for you to be off."

The little woman having found her fishing net, now empty but for the current number of "The Upper Ten Novelette," went carefully. Her sailor hat was slightly awry, and detecting this by a casual glance at some polished brass, she adjusted it, and pulled her cape straight. The circle of defending boys conducted her to the side of the ship; saw her safely down the slippery gangway ladder to the gig.

"I shan't kiss you, me dear," she whispered to Robert, "because they'd only guy you about it afterwards."

"Give my love to 'em in Pimlico Walk," said Robert shyly, as he lifted her into the boat.

"I shall keep some of it for meself," said the little woman archly. She spoke to the officer at the stern of the boat. "Which side of the boat shall I sit, mister?" The officer replied that it could not possibly matter. "Oh, well," she said resignedly, "if it overbalances don't blame me. Goo' bye, Bobbie."

"Goo' bye," cried Bobbie.

"Be a good boy," called out the little woman in the rocking gig.

"A good what?"

"A good man, I mean," she shouted apologetically.

"That's better."

"Don't forget," cried the little woman, putting one hand to the side of her mouth—"oh, dear! how this boat does bob about—don't forget that we mean to be proud of you."

"I shan't forget," he promised.

And, indeed, Robert Lancaster kept this in his memory.

## CHAPTER XV

Life on the Westmouth being too exacting to permit one to count the hours, Robert Lancaster came to the end of his training there with a sudden jerk that almost astonished him. Fifty lads were taken off the books, of whom he found himself to be one; some of them deciding for the merchant service, were despatched to the Home at Limehouse for that purpose; others, qualified in regard to measurement and desires, only waited for the brigantine to arrive for their names to be taken off the Watch Bill, and to resign their numbers to other lads. The old captain, meeting Robert on the upper deck, honoured him with five minutes' conversation, giving him a word of counsel, and directing him to give the old ship a call whenever the chance to do so offered.

"Don't forget, my lad, that now your opportunity is coming to show us all that the trouble and money you have cost have been well laid out."

"Yes, sir!"

"Keep yourself straight; be obedient to your officers, remember that the Navy has a fine, a glorious reputation, which you must help to keep up."

"Yes, sir!"

"Above all, be a credit to the Westmouth, and see that we have good news of you. That will do."

"Pardon, sir. Any objection to my having a day in London 'fore I join the—"

"To visit friends?"

"Yes, sir."

"If you please," said the old captain with his sharp air of courtesy.

See Robert Lancaster clearing his locker down on the lower deck and distributing souvenirs to his colleagues; a part of the inside of a watch to one; a copy of "Kidnapped" to another; several pieces of rare old string to the boy from Poplar, now, under the stress of Westmouth discipline, a contented, optimistic lad. See Robert Lancaster going off in the gig with six shillings tied in his handkerchief, being part of the prize for swimming gained by him at the last competition, and taking train at the small station for Fenchurch Street. See him arriving near the old neighbourhood and walking with a fine, sailor-like roll in his wide trousers and open-necked jacket towards Pimlico Walk, in which thoroughfare, now it seemed to him more preposterously narrow than ever, children stopped the playing of tipcat to stare at him open-mouthed, and women going into miniature shops arrested themselves in order to ascertain, from feelings of vague curiosity, his destination.

"No one about?" he asked in the doorway of Mrs. Bell's millinery establishment. The small window was still set out with magnificent feathered hats, but there appeared to be a suggestion of good taste in the arrangement that had in the old days been absent.

"Yes," said a little girl sitting on a high chair behind the counter, "there's me."

"No one else?"

"Who else d'you want?" asked the girl cautiously.

"Isn't Mrs. Bell about?"

"She's been bedridden for the last six months, if that's what you call being about."

"And Trixie?"

"You mean Miss Bell?"

"Miss Bell, then."

The girl stepped from the stool, and went to the foot of the stairs.

"Shawp!" she cried. She returned at once to the counter with a manner slightly less defensive. "She sits upstairs and reads to the old gel in the middle of the day, and I'm in charge down 'ere. When she comes down I go up, see? It don't do to leave the place without someone."

There was a rustle on the lower stairs.

"Bobbie!" A delighted exclamation.

"'Ullo, Trix," he said nervously. "How's the world using you?"

"'Aven't you grown?"

"You've been at that game, too. I s'pose I was about the last person that was in your mind."

"Yes," said Trixie Bell, "the very last. Me and mother were just then talking about you upstairs. Isn't your face brown, too?"

"Yours isn't brown," said Robert, with a clumsy attempt at compliment, "but it's got every other good quality."

"'Tilderann," commanded Trixie Bell, insistently, "go upstairs and sit with mother at once, and tell her that Mr. Lancaster has called." The little girl slid from the high stool again and disappeared reluctantly. "Up the stairs, I said," remarked Trixie, looking round the corner after her, "I didn't ask you to wait on the second step listening."

Miss Bell returned demurely to the inner side of the counter.

"Girls," she said, with an air of maturity, "want a lot of looking after."

"Who looks after you?" asked Bobbie, leaning over the counter.

"Oh, I can take care of myself."

"For one day, at any rate, I'm going to take care of you. Give me a kiss."

"Bobbie! People can see through the shop window."

"You won't give me a kiss?"

"There's a time," said the pleasant-faced young woman, with great preciseness, "and a place for everything, and this is neither the time nor—"

One advantage of being trained as a British sailor is that you can vault over a counter and jump back again before anyone has time to protest.

"You'll make me cross," said Trixie, with great confusion and delight.

"Give it back to me, then," suggested Robert.

"I fancy I see myself doing that," said Trixie, ironically.

"I've fancied it a lot of times," remarked Robert. "Now it seems to me we've arrived at what you may call reality."

"Of course," said Trixie, leaning on the counter and keeping one eye on the window, "it isn't exactly as though we were strangers, is it? What I mean to say is, we've known each other, Bobbie, for a long time, and you'll be seventeen next birthday—"

"Don't argue," said Robert. "Do what I ask you."

"It'll 'ave to be a very little one," said Miss Bell, seriously. And leaned forward.

"Thanks," said Robert. "That's what I've been looking forward to."

"Now, you must give up all this nonsense," declared Trixie, with a sage air, and glancing at herself in the panel looking-glass, "and behave. Will you come upstairs and see mother?"

"I thought p'raps you and me might go out this afternoon for a bit of a outing. I've got to rejoin my ship this evening, and I shan't have many chances of seeing you when I'm down at Plymouth."

"There's something in that," admitted Trixie. "I'll see if I can get a lady friend of mine from Pitfield Street to look in for a few hours." She raised her voice and called at the foot of the stairs. "'Tilderann! Come down this minute."

The girl obeyed, remarking in a grumbling undertone that the place was a perfect treadmill, and that for her part she envied the folk in Pentonville; she went to the doorway and reproved two infants outside for breathing on the glass, in good, well-chosen, and effective terms.

"Don't put your arm round my waist, Bobbie," whispered Trixie as they went up the dim, narrow staircase. "Besides, there's a buckle on my belt. Mother, 'ere's a gentleman come to call on you."

Mrs. Bell, raising her head from the white pillow, gave a chuckle of recognition. Robert, with his cap off, made his way round the bedstead, which seemed nearly to fill the room, but not quite, and shook hands with the large invalid.

"My poor old 'ead," she remarked, jovially, "gets in such a fluster, sometimes, that I can't remember nothing, and when the gel said Mr. Lancaster was in the shop it took me minutes to think who she meant. D'you think Trixie's growed?"

"Growed up and growed 'andsome," said Robert. Mrs. Bell gave a sigh of content, closing her eyes for a moment. "And how are you, ma'am? On the mend, I 'ope."

"Oh," said Mrs. Bell, opening her eyes and speaking loudly, "I've got nothing to complain of." She lowered her voice, and added confidentially, so that Trixie should not hear, "May pop off at any moment."

Trixie having explained the proposal that Robert had made, suggested that she should go round now to engage the services of the millinery friend in Pitfield Street. Her mother agreed cheerfully.

"Of course," said the old lady in a very loud tone, "I've been used to a active life, and naturally enough it goes somewhat against the grain for me to be kep' in one room for monce and monce. Otherwise I feel as well—" Trixie went out of the room, closing the door, and Mrs. Bell stopped and winked solemnly. "It'd never do to let her know the truth," she whispered. "I always like to pretend before her I'm getting better. It's a rare game sometimes the dodges I 'ave to get up to so that she shouldn't know how bad I am."

"Trixie isn't a bad sort," remarked Robert.

"She's my daughter," said Mrs. Bell.

Before that excellent young lady returned poor Mrs. Bell and Robert had a long, confidential talk. The cheerful old lady regretted that her time had arrived before Trixie had become a grown woman, but this regret was tempered by confidence in her daughter, and by a promise which had been given by Miss Threepenny to come and live with Trixie when all was over. There breathed pride in the statement that her doctor from New North Road could find no English name for her illness, and had been compelled to fall back on the Latin tongue to give it title; Mrs. Bell's old head trembled with gratification as she told Robert of this.

"D'you mind 'olding my 'and, Bobbie?" she asked, interrupting herself. "I feel so much more contented somehow when someone's 'olding me 'and. Thanks! As I was telling you—"

The doctor had some time since recommended that she should be taken away to the seaside, a procedure which might prolong her life for a few months, but the old lady congratulated herself upon having had the shrewdness to reply that Hoxton was as good a place to die in as any other, and that she had not been saving money all her life in order to spend it foolishly on herself at the end. The good soul seemed quite happy; everybody, she said, was very kind to her, and Trixie, who in former days had been somewhat masterful towards her, now waited on her "hand and foot." Mrs. Bell declared that she only wished everybody could be looked after at the end of all as effectively. Trixie, returning with her substitute, came upstairs in a hat which Robert, on being appealed to for an opinion, declared looked like ten thousand a year, and they said good-bye to Mrs. Bell, Trixie promising to send up 'Tilderann and to return herself at the earliest possible hour.

"Don't 'urry," said the old lady. "And, Bobbie! Come back one moment. Trixie, you go down." Robert obeyed. "I shan't be seeing you again," said the old lady brightly. "If so be as I should meet your poor mother, I shall tell her what a fine lad you've growed to." Robert bent and kissed the large white face. "Be good, won't you," she whispered brokenly, "to her?"

"You can make yourself quite sure about that, ma'am," said Robert.

Before going west on this sunny afternoon, the young lady insisted that Robert should accompany her for a short tour through certain streets in Hoxton, where her lady acquaintances resided, which same young women told each other afterwards that they had not realized what the word pride really meant until seeing Trixie with her young man. They looked at Ely Place from the dwarf posts at the Kingsland Road end, where towzled-hair, half-dressed, grubby babies played games with mud and swore at one another, but the two agreed that they had no desire to go through the Place. One more girl acquaintance in a Hoxton street shop in whose sight Robert had to be paraded, and then the two young people, walking down into Old Street, took a tram for Bloomsbury.

"You pay for yourself," said Trixie Bell definitely, "I'll pay for myself."

"No fear," protested Robert, "I pay for both to-day. This is my beanfeast."

"Then I go no further," declared the young woman. "Agree to that, Bobbie, or down the steps I go."

"You are obstinate," said Robert. "I never saw such a one for 'aving her own way."

"Not much use having anybody else's way," she said. "Bloomsbury, one," she said to the conductor.

The principle thus definitely laid down being adhered to during the afternoon, Robert found himself unable in consequence to assume the air of condescension and patronage that he had promised to wear; indeed, Miss Bell took the entire management of the afternoon into her own hands, with a quaint air of decision which surprised Robert and interested him, so that when at the end of the tram line she said, "Regent's Park," it was to Regent's Park they went; on Robert in his reckless way suggesting a 'bus, she said, "Walk, it's no distance," and that was the mode of transport adopted. In Regent's Park they sat on chairs near to sweet-smelling oval bouquets of flowers, watching the white-sashed nursemaids and the children, and whilst Robert (to Trixie's content) smoked a large, important cigar, she chattered away about her plans for the future. Trixie revived the old ambition of a milliner's establishment, with French words in white letters on the window, in some position not too far distant from Pimlico Walk, so that old customers should be preserved, whilst new ones were being caught; Robert watched her admiringly as she sketched this magnificent project, noting the decision of her chin and the flush of interest on her attractive face. The cigar finished, or nearly finished (for Robert was not yet a confirmed smoker), they walked arm-in-arm through the gates to the upper portion of the park, where there were sheep to be looked at, and near to the fountain, small debating societies, that seemed to grow on the grass in the style of mushrooms, and were made up of grubby men, arguing, as it seemed, on every topic of which they were ignorant, with here a reference to John Stuart Mill, and there satire at the expense of Apostles. Near to one of these groups Robert and Trixie stopped.

"As for your so-galled Queen, my goot Anglish friends," a foreign gentleman with no collar shouted in the centre of the mushroom, "it don't dake me long times to gif you my obinion about her and all her plooming Gofernment."

"Now you're beggin' the question," said his opponent. "Let's keep to the point at issue. If you've ever read Plito, you would have been aware that—"

"I'm not dalkin' about Blato," said the foreigner, with excited gesture. "I'm dalkin' about the bresent day and the stupid, foolish idea that you Anglish are a free nation. My obinion of your Queen, my fellow, is simply these. She's—"

Not quite clear what the foreign gentleman wanted to say, and impossible to hear what he did say, for at that moment a sailor lad edged his way through the crowd, two brown hands seized the neck of his collarless shirt, and at once the two—Robert and the foreign critic—were running away pell-mell to Gloucester Gate, the foreigner forced to go at a good pace despite his struggles, and being thrown eventually well into the roadway outside the park. Robert returned to Trixie a little heated with the run; Trixie's blue dotted blouse danced with delight and admiration.

"That'll learn him," said Robert, darkly.

In the Zoological Gardens they walked through the long house where lions and tigers lodge, and Robert kissed Trixie in full sight of a very sulky old lion, who had a bed-sitting room near to the end, making the lion use an exclamation of annoyance and envy that cannot well be printed. Then they went out into the gardens to see long, thin, ridiculous legs with birds perched riskily atop, and had a long conversation with one of the highly-coloured parrots, who were all talking at once, and seemed, like the debaters outside, to be denouncing somebody, and in similarly raucous voices.

"At tea, Bobbie," said Trixie, with a touch of her decisive manner, "I want to talk to you."

"You've been doing that the last hour or two," he said, good temperedly.

"Ah, but I mean seriously," she said.

At tea on the gravelled space near to the sleepy owls Robert encountered friends whose presence deferred the weighty talk, friends in the person of the angel from Folkestone, now clearly Mrs. Customs Officer, her husband and a large-eyed astonished baby in a white beef-eater hat. The angel came over from her table on recognizing Robert and declared that the news of this meeting would do poor uncle more good than all the embrocation in the world.

"Allow me," said Robert with importance, "to introduce my"—he coughed—"fiancée."

Trixie on this introduction assumed a distant manner, and sat alone with a reticent air, while Robert went over to speak to long Mr. Customs, and to dance the amazed infant high into the air. The angel had grown very matronly; the Customs seemed to be well under her control, insomuch that he never commenced a sentence without finding himself instantly arrested and brushed aside by his wife. On Robert rallying the angel on this, the angel laughed good-humouredly, declaring that it was well for one or the other to be master, and prophesying that some day Robert would find this out for himself, whereupon Robert insisted that women must not be too tyrannical, and endeavoured to enlist the Customs on his side in the argument, but the Customs shook his head vaguely (being it seemed with no grievance to complain of), and begged not to be dragged into the discussion.

"What name was it you called me just now?" demanded Trixie, when he had returned to her. Robert explained, and Trixie's young forehead cleared. "That reminds me," she said, resting one small shoe on the bar of Robert's chair, "I want to talk sense now."

"Why?"

"I want you," she said slowly and carefully, "to promise me—"

"I'll promise anything you like."

"To promise me that you'll give up all idea of being a sailor, and take up some occupation on land."

Robert shifted his chair and Trixie's foot slipped to the gravel. He re-tied his lanyard with great particularity, humming a tune. Trixie, fearful of the reply, drew a heart with the ferrule of her parasol on the gravel.

"Not me!" he said decidedly.

The heart on the gravel found itself rubbed out sharply and rendered illegible.

"You think it over, dear," said Trixie Bell.

"I shan't think it over," replied Robert Lancaster sturdily. "It'd be a mean trick to do after all they've spent on my training."

"I don't see how it would affect them."

"I'm not going to do it, Trixie."

"So long as you earn a honest living—"

"Look 'ere," burst out Robert impetuously, "I can't argue with girls. My mind's quite made up, and I'm not going to alter it."

"That means, then," said Miss Bell, swallowing something, "that you don't care for me."

"It don't mean anything of the kind," protested Robert. "It's a question of duty."

"You'd easily get a good berth on shore," she argued, "and earn good money, and then we could see each other pretty of'en. As it is, I may not see you from one year's end to the other."

"Absence makes the 'eart grow fonder."

"Yes," said the young woman pointedly, "in books."

"Well," remarked Robert, after a pause, "now that we've cleared up this argument, 'ave some more tea."

"No, thank you," said Trixie with reserve. "I think I must be getting along 'ome. Looks as though we shall 'ave a shower presently, I think."

"Trixie," he said, trying to take her hand, "don't be a young silly."

"After that complimentary remark," she said rising, "it's most certainly time for me to be off. To be told in the Zoo above all places in the world that I'm a silly—"

"I didn't say you was a silly," urged Robert with great perturbation, "I asked you not to go and be one. Do stop, and let's be good friends the same like—"

He was following the indignant young woman when the waiter interposed, offering a delicate hint to the effect that his services were usually deemed worthy of reward; by the time Robert had found threepence Trixie had disappeared in the direction of the camels. Other visitors watched the hurried distracted efforts of the scarlet-faced sailor lad on his erratic voyage of discovery with as much interest as though he had been an escaped resident of the Gardens.

A gloomy young man strode down Great Portland Street an hour later, and, losing his way more than once, because he was too much annoyed to speak to policemen, found himself at last in Holborn and eventually in Fetter Lane. On the two middle-aged ladies in the shop saying that Mr. Myddleton West was not in, and had indeed removed, Robert, muttering that this was just like his luck, turned away with a decision to return to Grays some two hours earlier than he had intended. On board the Westmouth one was at any rate free from illogical young women; free also from the irritating risk of taking wrong turnings. A swift hysterical shower of rain started.

"Beg pardon, sir," he said gruffly.

"My fault," remarked the man with whom he had come in collision. "I ought not to hold my open umbrella in front of me."

"Mr. West, I believe, sir."

"Young Hoxton!"

"That's me, sir."

"You look quite a man," said Myddleton West genially. "Come back to my office, and talk."

"You look ten years younger, sir, than when I see you last."

"I am ten years younger," said West. "On second thoughts we might eat. Do you feel like a good square meal?"

"I'm off me feed just for the present. Had rather a whack in the eye this afternoon."

"That's only a prelude to good luck," said Myddleton West, with new optimism. He seemed to be taking cheerful views of the world; appeared brighter than in the old days, and the lad felt inclined to resent it. "Providence is very fair in a general way."

Turning into a dim, insignificant passage off Fleet Street, they found a doorway, as if by accident, which led them (also, as it seemed, by a series of misadventures) to a square old-fashioned dining-room of the early Victorian type. Several men were seated at the wooden tables eating; two or three Americans with note-books were being supplied by one of the old waiters with a quantity of new and incorrect information about the old eating-house, enlivened by rare anecdotes of celebrities. In five minutes there was set before West and Robert Lancaster a small mountain made up of admirable strata of pigeons, of oysters, and of steak. Robert began by gazing absently at the dish before him, and thinking about Trixie; the smell of appetizing food changed his thoughts, and he presently set to with admirable appetite.

"My great news can easily be told," said Myddleton West across the table. "I was married last week."

"Good business!" remarked Robert. "Who is the lady, sir?"

"There is but one."

"But I thought she'd decided—"

"They never do that," remarked West.

"She used to like talking about you, sir, to me when I was in the hospital. I always thought it would 'appen some day."

"I'm ordered out to some God-forsaken place in Siberia," said Myddleton West. "They are making a new railway, and there's a lot of excitement, I believe. Miss Margaret was good enough to insist upon marrying me, before I went. When I come back my wife will give up her nursing business and we are going to settle down and enjoy life."

"Good deal to be said for the old fashions," said Robert wisely. "Independence is all very well, but I don't like to see it carried too far. Not with the ladies at any rate," he added.

"Tell me all about yourself," urged Myddleton West. "My wife will be anxious to hear. My wife," West seemed proud to repeat these two words, "was always interested in you."

Robert felt distinctly better when he had come out into Fleet Street and had said a respectful good-bye to Myddleton West; this partly because of the excellent meal and partly because of the friendly chat. The shower had finished and he walked East. Not until he had nearly reached Fenchurch Street, with only five minutes to wait for his train, did he remember that he had a high important grievance which careful attention would, as he knew, nurture into lasting remorse. He went slowly up the stairs of the station, and thinking with a desolate sigh of women in general and of Miss Beatrice Bell in particular. At the top of the staircase he caught sight (his look being downcast) of Miss Threepenny.

"Well, you're a nice young gentleman," said the little woman, satirically, "I don't think. Fancy coming to London and not waiting to see me. This," added the mite, with a twinkle in her bright bead-like eyes, "is what you call constancy, I s'pose."

"There's no such thing as constancy," growled Robert. "Not in this world, at any rate."

"Shows what you know about it," declared the little woman. "Come over 'ere; I've a friend I want to interduce you to."

"I've only got five minutes before my train goes."

"Five minutes is ample. Come along."

To the side of the bookstall Miss Threepenny convoyed Robert; once in harbour there bade him on no account to stir, and puffing off like a busy little tug to the waiting-room, returned immediately with that trim yacht Trixie Bell in tow, whom she also brought to anchor at the side of the bookstall.

"I'll go and see what platform your train starts from," then cried the little tug.

"Bobbie," said the well-appointed yacht, penitently, to the man-of-war, "I'm—I'm so sorry if I went and made myself look like a stupid this afternoon."

"Trixie," said the man-of-war, coming dangerously close to the side of the neat craft, "if anybody's to blame, it's me. Only—"

"We shall quarrel again, dear," said Trixie Bell, sedately, "if you talk like that. You're quite right in what you've made up your mind to do, and I respect you all the more for it, and if you're away ten seconds, or if you're away ten years, I shall always be the same and—"

The man-of-war saluted with so much promptitude that a newspaper boy in the bookstall, safe in ambush behind an illustrated journal, made ventriloquial comment. Miss Threepenny hurried up.

"Now run, Bobbie," said the tiny woman, breathlessly. "You'll just catch it, and—good luck to you!"

He caught the train as it moved out of the station and jumped into a third-class compartment. When he had regained his breath he leaned his bare head delightedly out of the window to enjoy the cool air that had come after the shower.

"Upon my word," he said, to Stepney Station, with some astonishment, "I begin to think that I don't half understand women."

From this remark it will be seen that Robert Lancaster, formerly child of the State, and shortly to enter the service of his great parent, was now no longer very young. Wherefore it is here that one may prepare to take leave of him.


## CHAPTER XVI

The new shop which bore the name of Miss Beatrice Bell stood so far up the Kingsland Road, beyond the canal, that you might have said it was in Dalston, and none would have dared offer contradiction. A happy situation, in that the shop found itself able to at once keep touch with the superior classes of Hoxton and with the middle classes of Dalston; a distinction being made in the two windows, so that Hoxton lady clients on entering turned instinctively to the left counter, whilst those from Dalston turned to the right. Beatrice Bell, grown to a tall, self-possessed young woman, still in slight mourning for her mother, had the nightly companionship of little Miss Threepenny, and assistance by day from the perky 'Tilderann, whose enthusiasm for the business was equalled by her intolerance of anything likely to interfere with achievement of these ends; her mistress's habit of buying evening newspapers whenever the placards shouted anything about the Delar expedition, of making customers wait while she read the telegraphic accounts nervously, constituted a weakness that made 'Tilderann groan. But for these occasional lapses Beatrice Bell had become a shrewd, business-like woman, not only reaching the high standard set by her assistant, but sometimes exceeding it, and extorting from that young woman gracious compliment. It was indeed worth watching to see and hear Miss Bell deal with some lady of Hoxton who having ideas of her own in regard to a new hat, insisted upon explaining them in detail. The young proprietress of the establishment would listen with perfect calm whilst the client described the kind of hat which represented her heart's desire; when she had finished, Miss Bell would say icily, "I quite understand what you mean, but," here a slight shrug of the shoulders, "they are no longer worn." Upon which the lady customer could only ejaculate a confused and abashed "Ho!" and request that something that was being worn should be taken from the window and exhibited to her.

Beatrice Bell, her hands clasped behind her, taking the air at the doorway of her shop, and bowing to acquaintances in the swift crowd of young women hurrying northward to their tea, glanced up and down the busy road with its sailing trams and jerking 'buses. The hour was seven; the sky still light with a juvenile moon that seemed, with the impatience of youth, to have come out too early. Dashing young blades of shopkeepers also taking the air at their doorways, caught sight of the white-speckled blouse, and bowed to her, and noting with pain her distant acknowledgment, declared to each other that Miss Bell would stand an infinitely better chance of getting married were she less reserved in manner, a drawback which had already cheated her of more than one invitation to Epping Forest on early-closing day. "For," said Mr. Libbis, the tobacconist, to his friend at the second-hand shop, "she may be as 'aughty as she likes, but after all, mind you, she's only a girl."

Opposite, a boy pasted on the boards outside the newspaper shop a new placard: "Brave conduct at Delar." She ran across the road to buy a copy of the newspaper; before she returned a customer came to the Hoxton side of the shop demanding something stylish at one-and-eleven. 'Tilderann fenced with her pending the return of her mistress.

"It occurred to me, looking in the glass," said the woman confidentially, "that I wanted smartenin' up. It may be only me fancy, but it struck me I was beginning to look old. What d'you think?"

"Depends what you call old," replied 'Tilderann. "Sure you can't run to more than one-and-eleven?"

"Eight year ago, or a trifle more," said the woman, reminiscently, "I was as light-'earted a young woman as you'd 'ave found in all 'Oxton, if you'd searched for a month. I was really the rarest one for making jokes that you ever 'eard of before my 'usband, Bat Miller, had to go away."

"Emigrated?" asked 'Tilderann, glancing between the hats and bonnets for her mistress.

"He were away," said Mrs. Miller, evasively, "for a matter of four or five year. And when I went to meet him, believe me or not, he was as stand-offish in his manner as he could he."

"That's like 'em," said 'Tilderann. "These bonnets at four-and-three are all the go just now."

"Quite 'igh and mighty if you please," went on Mrs. Miller aggrievedly. "And I firmly believe that if I hadn't had on my best mantle he'd have gone off again, goodness knows where. As it was, I persuaded him to settle down, and we've got on as well as can be expected; only that now and again, when we have a few words, he says something very satirical about the old days in Ely Place."

"Here she is!" said 'Tilderann. "Come on, Miss! 'Ere's a customer been waiting for howers."

"Sorry," remarked Beatrice Bell, panting. Her pretty face was crimson with excitement; she hugged a pink halfpenny journal to her breast.

"Something at about one-and-eleven, Miss," said Mrs. Miller respectfully. "Not too quiet and not too loud, and something that'll suit my features."

Miss Bell, trembling oddly, went up the wooden steps and brought down a box containing black hats.

"Anything special, Miss, in the evening paper?" asked Mrs. Bat Miller ingratiatingly.

"Yes," said Beatrice, panting.

"I of'en 'ave a look at the playcards," said Mrs. Miller; "they give me about as much information as I want. Are these the newest shape in this box?"

"Look at the corner of the box," said Miss Bell, endeavouring to regain her usual composure. "That'll tell you, 'Chapeaux de Paris.'"

"Sounds all right," agreed Mrs. Miller. "I was saying to your young lady here that I've been making up my mind to take more trouble about me personal appearance. Otherwise, it's likely enough Miller'll be getting tired of me again, and then there'll be more trouble. How would you advise me to have this trimmed, Miss, if it isn't troubling you too much?"

Beatrice Bell gave advice in a hurried way as though pressed with more urgent affairs, and anxious to see her customer depart. Mrs. Miller did go, after reciting some more of her personal history; when she had gone Miss Bell took the evening paper from her waistbelt and sat down behind the counter. She had scarcely done so when the bell of the door rang and a tall young woman came in, dressed in a tailor-made costume, which caused 'Tilderann to gasp with admiration.

"Will you," she said pleasantly to that amazed girl, "give the driver this half-crown and tell him not to wait?" She turned brightly to the young proprietress. "You are Miss Bell, are you not? My name is Mrs. Myddleton West."

"One moment," said Miss Bell trembling, "till the girl comes back, and we'll go into the shop parlour."

"You have read the evening paper I see."

"I've got it certainly, ma'am," replied the agitated young woman, "but as to reading it, why my eyes get so full the moment I begin that I can't get on with it very fast."

"I have a letter from my dear husband," said Mrs. Myddleton West proudly, "from my dear husband giving fuller particulars."

"And you've come straight here?"

'Tilderann returning, flushed with victory because she had compounded with the cabman for two shillings and two pence, and therefore able to refund the sum of fourpence, was commanded to look after the shop, and Miss Bell conducted her visitor into the small room at the back. 'Tilderann, noting with regret that the door closed carefully, found compensation in serving across the counter imaginary bonnets to imaginary wives of society millionaires at the price of fifty guineas per bonnet.

"Is this Robert Lancaster?" asked Mrs. West in her pleasant way. She took up a photograph of a brown-faced sailor lad, clean shaven, with a humorous mouth and bare neck.

"That's my Bobbie," said Beatrice Bell with pride. "Won't you take the easy chair, ma'am? It's been quite a lovely summer, hasn't it? I suppose we shall soon have autumn upon us if we're not careful, and—Oh," she cried, interrupting herself. "What is the use of me pretending to be calm when I'm all of a tremble!"

"Now you must sit down," this with a kindly authoritativeness, "sit down here close to me, and I am going to read to you the letter from my husband, which arrived only this evening."

"From Delar?" asked the girl, seating herself obediently on a hassock.

"From Delar."

"How could you let your husband go away, ma'am?"

"I don't think I can," said Mrs. West, "again." She found the letter and took the thin sheets carefully from the envelope. "But I felt that I ought not to be selfish all through my life."

"Weren't you the sister who looked after Bobbie in the hospital, ma'am?" Mrs. West nodded and smoothed out the sheets of note paper. "I wasn't quite sure whether Mr. West wouldn't go and marry some one else, considering—I s'pose I've no business to say so—but considering the way you kept putting him off."

"I took care," said Mrs. Myddleton West quickly, "that he should not do anything so absurd. Shall I begin the letter?"

"If you please, ma'am," said Beatrice Bell, looking up respectfully. Mrs. Myddleton West commenced.

"My dearest, ever dearest," she stopped. "I don't think I need trouble you with the first page at all," she said with some confusion.

"I know what you mean, ma'am. Start where he begins to speak of Bobbie."

It appeared that Bobbie came in about the middle of the second sheet. The war correspondent out at Delar had intuitively written on one side of the paper only, and Trixie Bell noted this deplorable want of economy, but West's small handwriting managed to convey a good long letter.

"You remember our young friend Bobbie Lancaster. The lad, now a sailor attached to H.M.S. Pompous, is on the launch where I am writing, and he did this afternoon an act of quiet bravery which ought, I think, to make his country feel that the trouble it took to make a man of him was not wasted. I am sending an account of the incident to my journal by the post which takes this letter to you, but you will care to have fuller particulars. How I wish that the mail were also taking me to the arms—"

"That," said Mrs. West, "is, of course, merely by the way."

"Skip a few lines," suggested Trixie, her chin resting upon her hands, "but don't leave out more than you're obliged."

The trail of the story was re-discovered.

"But touching Lancaster! We left H.M.S. Pompous and steamed up a broad smelly river, bordered by mangrove trees with long weeping branches, and approached the town of Delar. Delar is nothing like a town, but a mere collection of whitewashed huts around a large circular hut, where that genial person, the king of Delar, has hitherto lived. It was in this central hut that he caused to be massacred the Englishmen who, at his request, came some months since to confer with him on the subject of trade; our expedition is, as you know, intended to prove to him that such tactics are not only unbusinesslike, but positively rude. This lesson will be taught him by our marines when they land to-morrow, and I have little doubt but that they will do it effectively. I was talking to the Intelligence Officer when Lancaster came up hurriedly, and, saluting, said that the Admiral wished to see the other officer at once. The Intelligence man hurried below, and Lancaster and I had two minutes' chat. He has grown a fine strong fellow, with honesty in both eyes, and muscular arms tattooed with the word 'Trix.'"

"The dear boy!" burst out Miss Bell.

"We talked of the old days, and he said that he only cared to think of Hoxton now because his sweetheart lived there."

"You might read that part again, ma'am."

"He talked of the old days, and he said that he only cared to think of Hoxton now because his sweetheart lived there."

The girl gasped.

"Fancy his talking about me," she said delightedly, "all that distance off. Go on, ma'am."

"Whilst we were talking, commotion began on shore. Men were running up and down; boats were launched, the Intelligence Officer and the Admiral, escorted by four marines and four sailors, prepared to leave. Some whistling and giving of orders; the steamer slowed and stopped. The Admiral, I may tell you, is a big-bearded fellow, daring, and very popular with the officers and the men, but on board the Pompous, just before we left, there had been general agreement that he had done a risky and almost a foolhardy thing in agreeing to a palaver with some of the king's supporters. The officers knew that his idea was to punish the king and the king only; whereas the officers desired to punish everybody. If you had seen the mutilated body of an English gentleman bound upon what is called a crucifixion tree near the king's hut, I think, dear, you would have agreed with the officers.

"Not being allowed to go on shore, I give most of the rest as recounted to me by my friend the Intelligence Officer. The Admiral and his escort descended into the boats and were rowed ashore by the natives; Robert Lancaster was one of the bluejackets. At the shore they were received with great courtesy by the king's chief ministers; the king, as we knew, had scuttled off inland on receiving news of our approach. With exceeding ceremony the Admiral and his escort found themselves conducted to the king's compound, the while on the launch our Maxim stood ready to rake the town on the least sign of treachery. At each door of the king's house lay a woman's dead body. This, it was explained, had been done to prevent the arrival of the English; a precaution on the part of the king that had proved singularly unsuccessful. In the palaver house, a long half-roofed building with a bronze serpent at the entrance, and inside, seats of dry red mud, the Admiral took up position, and through the interpreter addressed the chiefs; Robert Lancaster being, as I am told, one of the men stationed behind the Admiral and his officers. Standing at a rough table the Admiral said that the great White Queen was angry because of the infamous massacre of her children; as a good mother she had determined to avenge their murder. But though the great White Queen was powerful, she was also just, she wished to punish only those responsible. Wherefore the king was to be pursued and captured and dealt with severely, but those of the natives who were friendly would not be hurt, and would, indeed, be under British protection."

"I am now," said young Mrs. Myddleton West gravely, "coming to the very serious part of the letter."

"May I hold your 'and, ma'am?" asked the girl. For answer she found her right hand taken instantly with a quiet matronly manner that gave her confidence.

"As the Admiral spoke and the interpreter repeated each sentence, the ministers listened with attention and with plain signs of agreement. The younger men rose from the red mud seats and pressed forward. They began to speak confusedly; the Admiral held up his hand for order. One of the younger men smashed a square of looking-glass on the floor; at the same moment Robert Lancaster flung himself suddenly on a muscular black youth who had risen from the ground close to the Admiral, unseen by others of the escort. The blade intended for the Admiral's back caught in the fleshy part of Lancaster's arm; a swift struggle ensued between the two before the others realized what was happening. A sharp revolver shot from one of the officers settled the murderous young black; Lancaster sucked at his own wound, spat, stepped calmly back to his place."

"Now, now!" protested the wife of Myddleton West, breaking off tearfully, "you mustn't cry, dear."

"I know," sobbed Miss Bell.

"The others shared his composure; the Admiral himself never lost self-possession for a moment. He concluded the palaver as though nothing of moment had happened; went out of the house with his escort and down to the shore and re-embarked. Arrived here on the launch, the Admiral sent for Bobbie.

"'What is your name, my lad?'

"'Robert Lancaster, sir, of the Pompous.'

"'Are you hurt, much?'

"'Nothing to brag about, sir.'

"'Do you know that you saved my life?'

"'Well, sir,' said Bobbie with great respect, 'I'm not sorry to have paid back a bit of what I owe.'

"'Mr. West,' remarked the Admiral, turning to me, 'let the English people know something about this. I will look after the lad, but you, too, can do something.'

"The doctor tells me that the blade was poisoned at the tip—"

Beatrice Bell's hand tightened her hold, and the white speckled blouse stilled for a moment.

"And that Lancaster's smartness and resource alone saved the wound from becoming dangerous. Lancaster wants you to call on his sweetheart and tell her all about it, because for a few weeks he will not be able to write. I shall be home, my dearest, in less than a month, and when I see you—"

"That is all about Bobbie," said Mrs. Myddleton West, stopping. "What do you think of it all, dear?"

"I could no more," declared Miss Bell, "explain to you what I think, ma'am, than I could fly. I'm too thankful to talk much." The girl looked wistfully at the sheets of rustling note paper. "You'd think I'd got impudence," she said hesitatingly, "if I told you, though, what I've got in my mind."

"Tell me!"

"Why, I was just thinkin' how annoyed you'd be if I was to ask you to give me the part that concerns—that concerns my Bobbie."

Far from showing annoyance, Mrs. West cheerfully ordered the production of scissors; 'Tilderann being called, responded so promptly that suspicious persons might have guessed she had become tired of serving imaginary customers, and had been trying to listen at the doorway. Having brought the scissors, 'Tilderann was sent back again to look after the shop. Then the two women bent their heads near to each other, and dividing the letter carefully, judiciously, and very lovingly, the shares were allotted.

"My dear," said Mrs. West rising, "come and see me at the address on this envelope to-morrow evening, and let us talk it all over quietly. Come to dinner."

"Me?" asked the astonished girl. "Me at dinner in Kensington?"

"I insist upon it."

"I'm a good talker," stammered Miss Bell, "in—in an ord'nary way, but just now—I only wish my friend Miss Threepenny was here."

A call from 'Tilderann.

"But some day me and Bobbie will be able to tell you how much—" She bent her head to her friend's hand impulsively. Young Mrs. West kissed her on the cheek.

"Lot of use anybody bawling 'Shop,'" said 'Tilderann at the doorway ironically, "when no one don't take no notice. Why, you're crying! Whatever's the matter, Miss?"

"Matter?" repeated Miss Beatrice Bell with indignation. "Do you think I should cry if there was anything really the matter?"


William Pett Ridge – A Short Biography

William Pett Ridge was born at Chartham, near Canterbury, Kent, on 22nd April 1859.

His family's resources were certainly limited. His father was a railway porter, and the young Pett Ridge, after schooling in Marden, Kent became a clerk in a railway clearing-house. The hours were long and arduous, but self-improvement was Pett Ridge's goal. After working from nine until seven o'clock he would attend evening classes at Birkbeck Literary and Scientific Institute and then to follow his passion; the ambition to write. He was heavily influenced by Dickens and several critics thought he had the capability to be his successor.
From 1891 many of his humourous sketches were published in the St James's Gazette, the Idler, Windsor Magazine and other literary periodicals of the day.

Pett Ridge published his first novel in 1895, A Clever Wife. By the advent of his fifth novel, Mord Em'ly, a mere three years later in 1898, his success was obvious. His writing was written from the perspective of those born with no privilege and relied on his great talent to find humour and sympathy in his portrayal of working class life.

Today Pett Ridge and other East End novelists including Arthur Nevinson, Arthur Morrison and Edwin Pugh are being grouped together as the Cockney Novelists.

In 1924, Pugh set out his recollections of Pett Ridge from the 1890s: "I see him most clearly, as he was in those days, through a blue haze of tobacco smoke. We used sometimes to travel together from Waterloo to Worcester Park on our way to spend a Saturday afternoon and evening with H. G. Wells. Pett Ridge does not know it, but it was through watching him fill his pipe, as he sat opposite me in a stuffy little railway compartment, that I completed my own education as a smoker... Pett Ridge had a small, dark, rather spiky moustache in those days, and thick, dark, sleek hair which is perhaps not quite so thick or dark, though hardly less sleek nowadays than it was then".

With his success, on the back of his prolific output and commercial success, Pett Ridge gave generously of both time and money to charity. In 1907 he founded the Babies Home at Hoxton. This was one of several organisations that he supported that had the welfare of children as their mission.

His circle considered Pett Ridge to be one of life's natural bachelors. In 1909 They were rather surprised therefore when he married Olga Hentschel.

As the 1920's arrived Pett Ridge added to his popularity with the movies. Four of his books were adapted into films.

Pett Ridge now found the peak of his fame had passed. Although he still managed to produce a book a year he was falling out of fashion and favour with the reading public and his popularity declined rapidly. His canon runs to over sixty novels and short-story collections as well as many pieces for magazines and periodicals.

William Pett Ridge died, on 29th September 1930, at his home, Ampthill, Willow Grove, Chislehurst, at the age of 71.

He was cremated at West Norwood on 2nd October 1930.


William Pett Ridge – A Concise Bibliography

Minor Dialogues (1895)
A Clever Wife (1895)
An Important Man and Others (1896)
Second Opportunity of Mr Staplehurst (1896)
Mord Em'ly (1898)
Outside The Radius. Stories of a London suburb (1899)
A Son of the State (1899)
A Breaker of Laws (1900)

London Only. A Set Of Common Occurrences (1901)
Lost Property (1902)
Up Side Streets – Short Stories (1903)
Erb (1903)
George And The General (1904)
Next Door Neighbours (1904)
Mrs Galer's Business (1905)
The Wickhamses (1906)
Name of Garland (1907)
Speaking Rather Seriously (1908)
Sixty Nine Birnam Road (1908)
Table d'Hôte. Tales (1910)
Splendid Brother (1910)
From Nine to Six-Thirty (1910)
Light Refreshment (1911)
Thanks to Sanderson (1911)
Love at Paddington (1912)
Devoted Sparkes (1912)
The Remington Sentence (1913)
Mixed Grill (1913)
The Happy Recruit (1914)
The Kennedy People (1915)
Book Here – Short Stories (1915)
Stray Thoughts from W. Pett Ridge (1916)
Madam Prince (1916)
The Amazing Years (1917)
Special Performance (1918)
Well To Do Arthur (1920)
Just Open. Short Stories (1920)
Richard Triumphant (1922)
Lunch Basket – Tales (1923)
Miss Mannering (1923)
Rare Luck (1924)
Leaps And Bounds (1924)
A Story Teller – Forty Years In London (1923)
Just Like Aunt Bertha (1925)
I Like To Remember (1925)
Our Mr Willis (1926)
London Types Taken From Life (1926)
Easy Distances (1927)
The Two Mackenzies (1928)
The Slippery Ladder (1929)
Eldest Miss Collingwood (1930)
Led by Westmacott (1931)


William Pett Ridge also wrote a play titled "Four small plays".